Boo

Danielle Stewart

# Copyright Page

An Original work of Danielle Stewart.
Settling Scores Copyright 2014 by Danielle Stewart

ISBN-13: 978-1500178376

Cover Art by: Ginny Gallagher
Website: www.Ginsbooknotes.com

## *Other Books by Danielle Stewart*

Piper Anderson Series:

Book 1: Chasing Justice
Book 2: Cutting Ties
Book 3: Changing Fate
Book 4: Finding Freedom
Book 5: Settling Scores
Book 6: Battling Destiny

Piper Anderson Series Extras:

Choosing Christmas - Holiday Novella - Chris & Sydney's Story
Betty's Journal - Bonus Material (Suggested to be read after Book 4 to avoid spoilers)


The Clover Series:

Novella & Book 2: Hearts of Clover – (Half My Heart & Change My Heart)
Book 3: All My Heart
Book 4: Facing Home (July 2014)

## *Dedication*

To my Papa. Hearing the pride in his voice when he talks about my books literally keeps me writing some days. My Nana and Papa gave my sisters and me some of the best memories of our lives. They put extra magic in Christmas and summer felt longer when all of us gathered at the beach. I carry them with me today even though distance keeps us apart. I remember how they welcomed us into their family without a moments hesitation and when I write about unconditional love, thoughts of them are easily conjured up. Thank you Papa for not just being proud of me, but for making sure I never forget it. I can't wait to make more memories on the Cape some day soon.

## *Synopsis*

Willow has been saved from a painfully dark past and handed a bright future. By all accounts, she should be happy. But no one seems to understand that escaping evil hasn't left her feeling free of it. The more people try to hold her close, the harder she fights to get away. Even the unconditional support from Edenville isn't enough to help her keep her head above water.

On a journey to settle scores and find answers to questions that haunt her memories, Willow hopes to mend her heart.

Meanwhile, the man she has pushed away time and again fights to show her the only chance she has at happiness is opening her heart to the love that is right in front of her. But even Josh's loyalty has its limits; how long before even he gives up on her, considering she's already given up on herself?

# *Prologue*

Everyone hates me. I'm not being melodramatic for effect. It's a reality. I think the only thing worse than being hated is not being self-aware enough to realize it. I am aware. Dotted across the country like attractions on a road map, there are people who think I'm scum.

If you went back to Block Island where my adoptive parents live, you'd see how the truth about my past spread like wildfire. I'd be willing to bet the money I stole from them, gossip is rolling its way over every sand dune and through every telephone line on the small and insulated island. My very respected parents are probably inundated with phone calls from people wondering why they would adopt a girl like me. A girl who spent the first part of her life in filth and chaos, marked to be sold into the abyss of trafficking by her biological parents. How could they make the conscious choice to allow someone like me into their lives, or onto their idyllic island? By now, they've heard my brother killed for me. I'm sure they're afraid I am just as violent or damaged as he was.

I don't have to look far to find more people that despise me. Take the ferry ride and travel to New York City and there is another group who can't stand me. The friends of my ex-boyfriend, Brad Angelo are all probably falling over each other as they talk about how awful I am. They, too, know my roots and in their circles that makes me unworthy. Brad likely returned from tormenting me and received a hero's welcome from his buddies.

Head down south to Edenville, North Carolina and I'm sure my name is synonymous with trouble. My crazy ex-boyfriend followed me into town just in time to ruin a wedding and slander me in front of everyone. I got painted a thief and a liar, and I'm too damn stubborn to stick around long enough to prove them wrong. In fact, I go with the philosophy that if they already think you are, you might as well be. I abandoned my brother as he transitioned out of jail. Worst of all, like an idiot, I fell for a guy I have absolutely no business being with, and then promptly stomped on his heart as I hightailed it out of town. Josh deserved better than that. Everyone there deserved better than I gave them.

So yes, anywhere I've been, I won't be going back. At least here in California I'm alone. It's just me and what I've come out here to do. I'm no one's victim. I'm no one's charity case. For the first time, I'm not trying to be what I think people expect of me, or what they insist I should be. Out here, I'm just a girl on a mission, one I've nearly completed. I'm on the verge of doing exactly what I came out here to do. So why do I still feel like shit? Would everyone still hate me, if they knew how much I hate myself?

## *Chapter One*

Willow pulled the black wig snug onto her head and shifted it slightly from side to side to make sure it was straight. She'd been wearing it for so long now that it was like second nature. There was something comforting about being in disguise. Hiding behind some heavy black eyeliner and covered in henna tattoos, she felt as though she were wearing armor. Slipping in and out of this fake identity had been necessary over the last few months, but she was starting to blur the lines between which personality felt more real to her. Was she Willow, the beat on confused mess who kept stepping in shit everywhere she went? Or could she be Claudia, the dark and desensitized runaway who'd partnered with a drug dealer to get revenge? Strangely, Claudia was becoming far more defined in her mind than Willow was.

Claudia was one-dimensional, whereas Willow was complex. Willow had been a victim. She'd been a reluctant survivor. She'd been transformed into the child of a privileged and loving family. After high school, she felt suffocated and unworthy of them so she broke away from that bubble. Her hair streaked purple, piercings and music all became who Willow was. But none of it felt right. She was messy and undefined. And she was exhausted with herself, just like everyone else seemed to be.

Willow slipped a black tank top over her head and pulled on her boots as she thought through the idea of becoming Claudia permanently. She took stock of how fleeing to Edenville on the heels of Brad's attack was a necessity. She hated herself for running toward the shelter of her brother's arms again, but she didn't know what else to do. Even though she was tormented by the guilt and confusion of her brother killing for her, she also knew he was the only person who'd be willing to do anything to protect her, just as he always had. And though she hated herself for needing it, she loved him for providing it. In many ways, he'd saved her again, not just from Brad, but from herself. Unfortunately, she couldn't be what Jedda wanted her to be. She couldn't stop being angry at the world long enough to let him in.

Leaving Edenville, Willow knew where she needed to go. California. She knew what she needed to do. Settle the score with Brad. It would be her way of standing on her own two feet and taking back her life. The problem was, she couldn't do it. But Claudia could. The edgy, strong, indifferent character Willow had created in order to execute her plan was starting to look like a much more appealing personality than her own jumbled up mess. As she grabbed her guitar and headed down the four flights of stairs away from her apartment, she gave it thought. Maybe when all of this is done, when I've accomplished what I set out to do, I'll just stay Claudia. Someone who knows who she is, knows what she wants and doesn't need anyone else in her life. I can create her story, and in the process wash away my own.

The thought of the past and the future faded away as she remembered how important the here and now was. The twelve-block walk to the bar was just enough time to get her head straight. The hard work had already been done. She'd taken all the risks, made all the connections. The dominos were set up. Tonight was just about tipping the first one over and watching Brad pay.

She pulled open the old wood door of the dimly lit

smoky bar and reminded herself how close she was to victory. She should be feeling good.

"Claudia," Marcario called and waved her over to his table in the corner. That was the only way you approached him, if he indicated you were welcome. Otherwise, if you tried walking up to his table without that small motion from him, you'd be tackled by two of his men. Over the last few months, she'd become part of his inner circle. Not the way she'd planned to but the end result was the same and that was what was important.

"Hey Marcario," she sang as she kissed his cheek and slipped into the chair across from him. "Everything on track?"

"That's all you ever care about isn't it? You think about anything besides business?" he asked as he slid his large hand across the table and covered hers. She didn't recoil or slap him away. Her hand wasn't still tucked beneath his because she feared him, though he'd proven he was someone to be afraid of. It was the opposite of that really. She kept her hand there because she trusted him.

She wasn't intimidated by his appearance though intimidation was clearly the intention behind his muscular tattoo-laden arms. In fact there wasn't an inch of his arms that wasn't covered in swirling colorful ink. The weather out in California was always mild enough for him and his guys to wear plain white tank tops, hanging low over their too large blue pants. His shaved head and piercing black-brown eyes were dangerously attractive when paired with his devilishly sharp edged smile. Willow ignored all of it though because Marcario had done something to undermine his persona. He'd opened up to her and in doing so lost his ability to instill fear in her. He knew it and so did she.

"We've been working on this for months and it's going down today. Don't you think we should be talking business?" she asked, giving him the flick of her eyes she knew he loved. He might be a tough man, but she'd certainly begun to crack his code.

"I think we should be in my bed celebrating," he smirked, and released her hand, both of them already knowing her answer to that proposition. "But since you always shoot me down I guess we'll do it your way. I heard from my source this morning. Big Bo is delivering the package to your boy in a couple hours. Everything should go down from there."

"I can't believe we pulled this off," Willow stammered as the waitress dropped a familiar drink down in front of her. A tonic and lime. Willow wasn't a good drinker, meaning it rarely ended well when she got drunk. Fights. Flings. Things went bad. And she didn't think it would mix well with the dangers of the plan her and Marcario were working on. Having her wits about her would be key. It kept her from screwing up and likely from sleeping with Marcario.

"You pulled this off," Marcario stressed. "Everyone around here is scared shitless of me, but if they only knew what you are capable of, they'd be running for the hills."

Willow let out a breathy laugh as she took a sip of her drink. "I really appreciate how you helped me. I had no clue what I was doing when I got here. You could have killed me, left me under the Saint Charles Bridge and never looked back. You didn't have any reason to trust me, much less help me."

"You're cute," Marcario hissed as he clinked his

glass against Willow's. "And I just kept thinking any little white girl who has the balls to meet with me in the middle of the night with a bag full of money pitching the plan you did, is dangerous. I rather have that on my side than come up against you."

"Please, I wasn't brave. I was desperate. There's a difference."

"True, but it worked. You were right. If I wanted to eliminate my competition and you wanted to eliminate your asshole ex-boyfriend then this was the way to do it. They're both so damn greedy and arrogant. All we had to do was bring them together, mix in a little money and some drugs and boom, they walked right into the trap. I had my contact tip off the cops about the where and when it will go down," Marcario whispered as he leaned in toward Willow. "They'll pick them both up and it'll be the last we hear from either of them for a long time."

"Perfect. It looks like we might actually get rid of both of them." Willow sighed, forcing a smile that shouldn't be so hard to find considering the good news.

"And then what?" Marcario asked, raising a knowing eyebrow in Willow's direction.

"Then Brad gets exactly what he has coming to him and so does Big Bo. Neither one of them deserves to be walking the streets." Willow averted her eyes as she remembered the story Marcario had told her one night about how Big Bo had beat his cousin Gabriella half to death. She knew in that moment that telling him what Brad had done to her would help her cause. It gave them a common purpose. It was the moment she realized she didn't need to be afraid of him.

"I don't live by many rules in my life," Marcario reflected. "I'd never been considered a saint by anyone's standards, but men who put their hands on women don't deserve to live, let alone walk free. If this hadn't worked with Brad, I think I might have hunted the two of them down myself and taken care of them." Marcario's face fell stone serious and it acted as a reminder to Willow of who this man really was. His reputation was one of ruthless violence. His kindness toward her was a fluke, and she knew it was important to remember who she was dealing with.

"Well it's almost done now," Willow shrugged as she sat back in her chair trying to seem calm and collected about the whole thing.

"Go sing while we wait," Marcario insisted. He was not shy when it came to getting what he wanted. The only exception was when he regularly professed his desire for Willow, well Claudia really, but they were halfhearted propositions. He wasn't foolish enough to think she'd ever live in his world or crazy enough to believe she'd be what he wanted.

But even if his attempts were hollow, one thing was genuine. His love of her voice. And she knew why. There were clearly dark moments of his life that were painted all over his body by way of scars. Slashes and jagged marks that told anyone who saw him, he'd been beaten. Ripped up knuckles that said he'd delivered beatings of his own. But her voice calmed him. In a way, it temporarily healed him and so she would get up on the small stage of the bar and sing. Even if no one else in the room cared to hear her, Marcario needed it, so she did.

"Sure." She smiled as she grabbed her guitar in one hand and rubbed his shoulder with the other as she passed. He was a sexy man, but she knew deep down as long as she was being smart nothing would ever happen between them. He'd become her partner, but it was a healthy respect for each other's end game that kept this working. If she slept with him, there was a better chance that everything would fall apart.

She made her way to the stage, pulled up the stool and began to strum her guitar. It always made her smile to see Marcario's face when the first lyrics would escape her mouth. It was like an addict getting a taste of a sweet drug. He'd lounge back and nod his head to whichever beat she was strumming. For a few minutes, a very complicated man looked like he didn't have a problem in the world. Knowing she was capable of giving him that small peace made her feel powerful.

As the hours passed, Willow felt her nerves fracturing. She needed to hear that all the risk she'd taken, all the time she'd put in was not in vain. Then finally Marcario's phone rang and he headed for the front door of the bar. Willow leaned her guitar against the wall and nervously followed him outside. She listened to a brief and coded conversation that took place between Marcario and whoever his contact on the other end of the line was. When he hung up, he tucked his phone in his pocket and nodded his head.

"You crazy bitch," he chuckled. "It's done. They caught them both dead to rights. Those two fools thought they were so badass that they were untouchable. Damn," he shouted, snapping his fingers sharply.

Willow sucked in a deep breath and fought back the urge to cry her eyes out. She was only partially successful as a lone tear trailed its way down her cheek. "Good," she said, biting at her lip to keep her chin from quivering.

"Game over," Marcario murmured, his dark eyes locking with hers as he moved with determination toward her. "You win." He brushed back her hair from her face and ran his thumb over the wet path her tear had blazed. Leaning in, he kissed her with heat and force she wasn't prepared for. It was the first time he'd ever touched her like this. She didn't pull away from him, nor did she lean in to him. She let him kiss her and to her surprise, after a moment, he softened. The hand he'd clutched to her cheek let up and brushed across the bone of her chin as he took a step back.

"Who are you really, Claudia?" Marcario asked, narrowing his eyes at her.

"Why?" Willow shot back, staring at her shoes and steadying herself. The kiss, combined with the probing question, had rocked her and she was trying to regain her grip.

"I know that's not your name, and I know you aren't some tough chick who doesn't care about anyone. Tell me who you are."

"Why?" Willow repeated, now meeting his eyes and ignoring the fact that hers were filling quickly with tears.

"Because part of me is wondering if you and I could run off somewhere and be preppy normal people together instead of this shit. Maybe you go back to your life and I come with you." Marcario sighed as he ran a finger from Willow's elbow down to the palm of her hand.

"I don't have any life to go back to and you wouldn't give up what you have here. Being the top guy, the money, and the power."

"You're right," he relented, running his hand over his shaved head. "But for some reason I still want to know who you are."

Willow brushed away the tears before they could fall and turned to head back inside to grab her guitar. "So do

I," she whispered, realizing even if she wanted to tell Marcario who she was, she wouldn't know where to start. If she knew the answer to that question, she likely wouldn't be here in the first place.

When she stepped back outside, guitar in hand, Marcario was leaning against the old brick wall of the bar sucking in a long drag of a cigarette.

"I thought you'd be happier than this. Isn't this what you wanted, Brad going to jail?" he asked, a puff of smoke billowing between his lips.

"I thought I'd be happier than this, too," Willow admitted as she adjusted her guitar case under her arm. It was the story of her life, she thought to herself.

"That means you're not done. Don't tell me there is something out there worse than Brad. Something else you're chasing. You're on your own for that. I can't get caught up in any more of your shit." He had a look on his face that let her know that wasn't true. If she asked, he would help her. They both knew it.

"I don't want to be chasing it, but I can't get some things out of my head. There was a time in my life when I saw things, and I wonder if I could have done more. I can't stop wondering."

"And you think you're going to do something about it now?"

"I have no clue," Willow sighed as she stared up at the sky. "I thought this was going to be it. I thought settling this would make me feel…"

"All healed?" Marcario laughed as a puff of smoke escaped his sinister smile. "Good luck kid. You can't undo things you've done. Trust me."

"You would if you could?" Willow asked, throwing him a sideways look. "You have regrets?"

11

"Look at me," he scoffed, tossing down his cigarette and stepping assertively toward her. "You think anyone really wants to live like this? Always looking over their shoulder? Always wondering if their mother's house is going to get a pipe bomb tossed in the window, or if their nephew is going to catch a bullet because of some twisted retribution shit. Yeah, I've got regrets."

"So get out. With your competition out of the picture in six months, you'll have more money than you probably ever had. Grab your family and go."

"You might not know who you are, but I know who I am." Marcario chanted as he pounded on his own chest. "I was born here. I'll die here. And not of old age." Marcario leaned in close to Willow as if he might kiss her again. "Be glad you don't know who you are yet. It means you have a chance to still be something good. Brad can't hurt you anymore. He can't hurt anyone you care about. Maybe you should start looking at what's ahead of you instead of what's behind you."

"If I thought I could outrun it, or force it out of my head, I would." Willow spoke down toward her shoes afraid to tip her head back and imply she was welcoming another kiss. She didn't love Marcario. His passionate kiss paled in comparison to what it felt like when her lips had met Josh's. But tonight she was lonely. She was exhausted and disappointed in herself, in how she was feeling. If he tried to kiss her again, she didn't think she'd have the willpower to stop him. She'd be following him back to his place, and she'd add to the pile of regrets and stupid choices she'd made over the years. So all she could do was stare at her boots, and pray he'd spare her.

"Then face it and move the hell on. Go be something great. Go sing for people. Use your voice to make them feel the way you make me feel when you sing." As his lips inched closer to her downturned face she reached into her bag and pulled out a CD she'd made. She knew there was a chance this would be the last time she saw Marcario and she wanted to leave him a piece of herself. The part he loved. Her music.

"Here are some songs, the ones you like the best."

"How do you know which ones I like the best?" he shot back as he took the CD from her and acted as though this gift didn't mean the world to him. His tough guy bravado wouldn't allow honesty in this moment.

"I can see it in your eyes when I sing. Marcario," she hesitated as she drew in a deep breath, "you can still get out if you want to. It's never too late. You could be something great too. Don't stay in this life if it's not what you want."

He leaned in, kissed her forehead and pulled her in for a tight hug, one she wasn't expecting. Did gang members usually hug? He was full of surprises tonight. "You're wrong, but it's nice to know someone thinks that about me. Now get out of here before I kiss you in a way that makes you drop that guitar and forget what day it is."

Willow felt an ache spreading through her heart. Marcario was a complicated man, but he'd been kind to her. A friend and an ally when she didn't think she wanted or needed one. He'd treated her like family and leaving him tonight was like walking straight into loneliness. Daunting, but she knew the alternative. Just like she'd become what her adoptive parents expected, and what she thought Brad wanted, she would quickly become who Marcario wanted, even if he wasn't trying to make that happen. She'd fall into his lifestyle; she'd lose any chance of really finding herself if she got lost in him for the sake of comfort.

"Goodbye Marcario," she mouthed as she walked backward a few steps before turning and hustling away. She needed the extra speed to maintain the courage to leave him.

As she headed back to her apartment, she knew what she had to do next. If she couldn't silence the past that was fighting its way into her mind then she'd have to face it head on. She'd already started the road map; maybe it was time to follow it.

Stopping at the liquor store was impulsive, not strategic. Willow had pulled the wig from her head and run her fingers through her short blond hair to try to bring life back to it as she rounded the corner to her place. The bottle of rum was a nostalgic choice—her biological father's drink—and when she twisted off the top, memories flooded back. The spicy smell was often on his breath, even the shape of the bottle, which hadn't changed all these years later, brought her back to those days. Dark days.

She wasn't even to the top of the stairs of her apartment before she was taking the first swig. It had been a while since she'd gotten wasted, but tonight she wanted to sleep. Good sleep had been elusive lately, and tonight she knew she might need to help it along. It was easy to pretend this was a celebratory buzz she was looking for, but that wasn't true. This was about escaping, numbing. Getting Brad busted hadn't done it. The act didn't fill the hole like she thought it would. So tonight, she'd settle for the burning warmth of being drunk, which didn't take long.

As the room began to spin and she felt her eyelids growing heavy she flopped down onto the small wooden chair in the corner of the room. The apartment came furnished with a chair, a desk and a bed, which was all Willow needed. She could survive as long as she had a place to write music, sleep when she was able and research.

The research hadn't been something she planned for. It didn't start as much but the more her past bullied her brain the more the project had begun to take on a life of its own. It transitioned from a few pieced together memories in the margins of her notebooks to a full-scale collage of information pinned to her wall. Pictures. Notes. Websites. Phone numbers. They were all taped and tacked up in an order that on a good day made her feel like she was getting somewhere. But today was not a good day. Today, the wall seemed to be taunting her. It reminded her that even an enormous amount of information means nothing if you don't do anything with it.

One phone number hadn't made its way to the wall. It was on a piece of paper that had been handled so many times it was beginning to tatter, the ink starting to smudge. She'd picked it up and then tucked it away so frequently that she was surprised it hadn't disintegrated yet. Looking down at the swirly scrawl of Betty's handwriting, she bit her lip. It had been slipped into her bag without her knowledge back in Edenville. It read simply, Josh. In case you need him. Followed by his phone number.

What amazed Willow was the fact that Betty hadn't known she was running off to California. She'd led them all to believe she was heading back to the comfort and isolation of Block Island with her parents. Would Betty still have left this note if she knew Willow was about to steal twenty thousand dollars from her college fund? Most people wouldn't have, Willow knew. Betty wasn't most people.

She picked up the shabby piece of paper and clumsily punched the numbers into her phone. As it began to ring, the spinning room seemed to increase its velocity, and she felt the urge to be sick. Josh's voicemail picked up as she stared at the wall she'd created. Taking in the information she'd been able to remember suddenly overwhelmed her. The long beep that indicated she should speak her message should have had her hanging up the phone, but instead, she was talking. Rambling really and she couldn't seem to stop herself. There weren't thoughts of the consequences or what Josh might think. She just needed someone to talk to, she needed to get it all out, and at that moment his voicemail was the best listener she had

.

## *Chapter Two*

Normally they'd all be sitting on the porch by now. It was Wednesday night, dinner at Betty's just finished, but tonight something was keeping them inside. As they gathered in the sitting room, Piper moved over and made a spot for Bobby on the couch. They all fell quiet as Bobby turned up the volume on the television. Piper looped her arm in his and leaned in her body against his firm shoulder. Even Betty was standing in the doorway of the sitting room, uncharacteristically neglecting the dinner dishes in order to hear the news broadcast Michael had called them all in for.

They sat with wide eyes and shaking heads as the reporter on the national evening news broke the story. Brad Angelo, son of Thomas Angelo, one of the most prominent lawyers in New York City, had been arrested last night for possession of a large amount of boutique drugs with the intent to distribute. The twist in the story was that the drugs were of the same chemical makeup that had been taken by Joel Silverrun, son of Senator Tom Silverrun. Joel had suffered brain damage as a result of the toxic compound. In turn, Brad would now be investigated for involvement in that case as well. He was being held without bail and his father could not be reached for comment, the anchor continued.

"What on God's green earth is a boutique drug?" Betty asked with a perplexed look on her face. "Does it come with a fancy hat or something?"

"It's a synthetic process for making drugs that are tailored to be sold to the wealthy. They are no different than street drugs, really. They just have a fancy name and marketing strategy that makes the rich people using them feel better about themselves. Shape that little pill like a heart, make it pink, and suddenly it's acceptable for socialites," Bobby explained, shaking his head in disgust.

"Is he really that stupid?" Piper questioned, looking over at Michael whose face was showing no reaction one way or the other. His courtroom glare, as Piper had come to know it. A lawyer couldn't be overly emotional if he wanted to be successful.

"How could he keep dealing after how close he came to you and Willow getting him in trouble for putting his friend in the hospital from poorly made drugs?" Jules asked, her voice high and annoyed.

"No, he isn't a stupid kid," Michael replied, shaking his head and motioning for Bobby to turn the television off. "But he is that arrogant. An arrest like that, involving so much narcotics, he won't be seeing the light of day for a long time. Not even his dad will be able to get him out of this."

"Good," Jedda grumbled, folding his arms over his chest. "He deserves to rot for what he did to Willow. The thought of his hand on her makes my blood boil. Letting him go, knowing he was out there has been driving me crazy. Now maybe this means Willow will go home, or even come back here."

"Still no word from her?" Jules asked as she propped Frankie up on her shoulder and patted her back gently. Piper looked with pure joy at her best friend and her Godchild –two of her favorite people on this planet. It was strange how far Piper had climbed out of the hole that was her old life. Now she was a part of something, and that something kept growing all the time.

"I haven't heard anything," Jedda reported with a shrug and looked over at Bobby in case he had any update.

Bobby squeezed Piper's hand as he spoke and she loved knowing he drew strength from her. The topic of Willow was contentious at times and he often relied on Piper for backup in the tough moments. "The phone we're tracking her on is still in use and still in the same area of Southern California. But her parents haven't heard anything from her either. I spoke to them a couple days ago and they're still very concerned. I've had to talk them out of sending a private investigator out to track her down. I told them she left here upset and that some space would do her good. But I can tell they're getting anxious to do something."

Crystal ran her hand across Jedda's stiff back and tried, as she always did, to find a silver lining. "I'm sure she'll hear the news about Brad and that will give her some peace. She might not go running home, but she could reach out to someone. We should be hopeful for that."

"I don't see why we can't just call the phone you're tracking. Maybe we can tell her the news." Jedda's voice was urgent as this familiar argument started up once again. It didn't come up every Wednesday night at dinner, but it was frequent enough and never resolved.

Bobby took his normal stance on it. "If she ditches that phone you could lose her for good."

Like usual Michael backed him up. "Spooking her would be worse than anything. She's out there trying to sort through how she feels. The best thing we can do is let her have space until she's ready to come around again."

As Jedda opened his mouth to argue, a very insistent knock on the front door drew everyone's attention. They looked from one to another each seeming to take mental inventory and coming to the same conclusion: We're all here so who could that be?

Betty stood and headed for the door, which was being pounded on again. Bobby was quick to her side and Clay behind him. "Who is it?" Betty called and they all waited nervously for a response. A tiny part of Piper prayed it was Willow.

"It's Josh, I need to talk to you." His voice was choppy and labored as though he'd run there from town.

"For the love of all things holy, Joshua Nelson, you had me as worried as a turkey in November. Knock like a normal person next time," Betty drawled, pulling open the door and promptly slapping Josh across the shoulder.

"I'm sorry, but it's important and I wanted to catch you while you were all together. It's about Willow."

"You heard the news?" Michael asked, stepping into the kitchen and shaking Josh's hand.

"What news?" Josh questioned, looking thoroughly perplexed. Piper sensed they weren't all talking about the same thing as she sidled up to Bobby.

"Brad. He's been arrested for a significant drug charge and it sounds like he's going to get put away for long time," Michael explained, but still Josh's face looked confused.

"That's what she must have been talking about," Josh mumbled, as he dug his phone out of his pocket. "She left me a voice mail in the middle of the night last night. I've listened to it all day today trying to figure out what she was talking about, what she needs."

"She called you?" Jedda asked, stepping forward with a demanding look on his face. "What did she say? Did she sound like she was all right? Why did you wait all day to tell us?"

"No. She did not sound all right," Josh admitted, ignoring almost all of Jedda's other questions. Instead, he pulled up the message and turned his phone so everyone in the room could hear it. Willow's voice began and immediately Betty's hand flew to her heart, protecting it from the ache in Willow's tone.

"I'm sorry it's so late," she slurred. "I don't know why I'm even calling. It's just I've been out here, trying to do this thing and now all of a sudden it's done. He's in jail. I did it. But I don't feel better. It was supposed to make me feel better. I'm staring at all these things on my wall and I should have done something. I should have helped them. I think I can help them now. I-I…" her voice cracked with tears. "I opened Pandora's box and it was too much. I remember more than I thought. Maybe that's what I have to do next. Maybe that's what will make me feel better…" Her voice trailed off as she whispered something incoherent and then the line disconnected.

"What the hell is she talking about?" Jedda panicked, as his eyes circled the room as though one of them may have the answer.

"I don't know," Josh admitted, as he tucked his phone away. "I mean I guess now I know the thing she went out there to do was get Brad arrested."

"That's not possible," Michael cut in. "What could she have done out there to get him arrested? She's not capable of orchestrating something like that."

Piper huffed out a laugh as she spoke, "I'd imagine you would have thought the same thing about me and what I was trying to do to Judge Lions. I don't think anyone would have expected I was capable."

"The other guy they named in Brad's arrest is a gang banger, a notoriously violent one on the west coast," Bobby explained, as he pulled up the information on the search engine on his phone. "He's based out of the same area Willow is in right now. Maybe she had more to do with this than we think."

"Did she get mixed up with them? I know she's as stubborn as an angry mule, but could she do that?" Betty asked, her brows furrowed with worry.

"She had twenty thousand dollars," Jules chimed in with a hushed voice as she bounced Frankie up and down rhythmically. "You can make a lot of things happen with that kind of money."

"What else could she be talking about?" Josh asked, shrugging his shoulders. "The timing is too much of a coincidence. Brad gets arrested and then she calls me and says all that. I think she was involved."

"If she would have been caught trying to do anything to Brad she'd be in violation of the non-disclosure agreement we signed with Thomas Angelo. I could have lost my license or ended up in jail," Michael asserted loudly, before quieting slightly at the wave of Jules's hand. "She can't be that self-destructive or care that little about what happens to other people. Does she really have no conscience?"

"I'm sure it's not that Michael," Piper snapped as she felt a pang of empathy ring through her. "Sometimes it's bigger than you think. You can't just shake it and move on. Brad hurt her, brought her back to a place and a time in her life she had buried away. I can't blame her for wanting to see him put away."

"I understand that," Michael seethed through gritted teeth, though his face was indicating he did not understand it at all. "I wasn't too pleased letting him walk free either. But occasionally, and I know this is hard for you all to understand, we have to act like adults. That can mean losing sometimes for the sake of self-preservation. I don't even want to imagine what she had to do or with whom she was associating with to pull this off."

"And it sounds like it's already done," Betty emphasized, calling a quick end to Michael's rant. "If she had anything to do with it then hopefully she's done. What I'm more worried about is this Pandora's box business she was talking about. She sounds like she's a wreck out there."

"I'm going to find her," Josh asserted, straightening his back and looking ready to fight the arguments against it.

Bobby was the first to react. "She doesn't really want to be found, Josh."

"I have the phone number she called me from. Can't you trace it? Just give me a location and I'll go get her."

"Me too. I'm going with you," Jedda said, looking like he could slip into his boots and be ready in sixty-seconds.

"Stop," Michael shot out, raising up his hands like he was directing traffic. "Jedda you can't go out there. You are on a short enough leash as it is. You're making incredible progress in your PTSD therapy and you've got a good thing going working at the restaurant. You have a routine and it's working for you. Breaking that now, going back into an emotionally charged environment with Willow, that isn't going to work. I've put my neck out for you and I need you to hear me on this."

Jedda looked away and nervously cracked his knuckles. "She's my sister. You heard her on that voicemail, she's a mess."

"I know and I don't disagree that someone should check up on her, I'm just saying it shouldn't be you. I'm sorry."

Crystal took Jedda's hands and calmed them in her own. "She'll be okay," she assured quietly.

"I'm going," Josh said again, this time even more definitively. "I'll make sure she's okay, I promise Jedda."

"Wait a second," Bobby cut in again. "What happens if you go out there and she bolts? What if she doesn't want to see you, doesn't want anyone to know where she is and so she takes off? She'll ditch the phone and we lose our only connection to her."

"She called me," Josh insisted. "That means something. I know it does."

"She sounded drunk," Bobby retorted, as though it discounted her call all together.

"Isn't that when people say what they really mean? I just need her location and I promise I won't scare her off." Josh's voice shifted from demanding to pleading.

"I don't see how you can make that promise. Nowhere on that phone call did she ask for your help."

"Bobby," Piper interrupted, putting her hand on his tense shoulder. "I never asked you to come to New York, but if you hadn't shown up in that alley, who knows what would have happened to me and Jules? You knew I needed you even before I knew it. We all need to be saved sometimes, even if we don't want to admit it."

"Careful girl," Betty sang through a smile, "you're starting to sound like me."

"There are worse things, Betty," Piper retorted, as she clamped her hand down tighter on Bobby's shoulder and winked at Betty.

He let the corner of his mouth curl up slightly as he spoke. "I don't know, two Bettys seems pretty scary to me." Everyone, excluding Josh, let out a small chuckle at the idea.

The room fell quiet as they all looked from one to another. Josh finally broke the silence. "I care about her and she called me. I think she needs some help." The heartbreakingly earnest look on his face caused a lump to grow in Piper's throat. Despite Josh's normally sweet demeanor, Piper could glimpse something fierce about him. And she couldn't help but root for him. He was likely Willow's best shot at coming out of the fog she was in.

"I'll give you the information we have tied to the cell phone," Bobby grudgingly relented. "But you have to be tactful. Don't go stomping in there and telling her she has to go home. That won't work with her. You have to be patient and give her space. If she feels pressured, she'll run. Life hasn't been easy on her, she's got a broken heart and the reflexes of a wild horse."

"You seem to know a lot about her," Josh said torn between wanting Bobby's opinion and telling them all to go to hell so he could get to Willow.

"I don't. But I have a lot of experience trying to love someone like that." Bobby wrapped his arm affectionately around Piper and looked down into her face.

"I'm sorry," Piper demanded, narrowing her eyes as she shrugged his arm off of her shoulder. "Did you just call me a horse?"

"No," Bobby stuttered, "I was saying you were skittish… You know what I mean. It wasn't easy."

"Loving me?" Piper asked, arching an eyebrow as

the room let out a low rumble of laughter. She let her face break into a smile as she turned toward Josh. "He's right. I'm giving him a hard time, but he knows what he's talking about. Everybody is different but I see a lot of similarities between Willow and me. Judging by that message, she's feeling like she's got to do something in order to feel better and that wasn't the case. Maybe you can convince her that real happiness doesn't come from some mission. It comes from the people you surround yourself with. It's not captured and kept in a jar. You have to let it go to see how amazing it can be."

"Someone get this girl an apron and stick her in the kitchen. She's Betty Jr.," Michael jested, scooping his daughter up and holding her high in the air as he made a silly face at her. Piper stepped forward and snatched the baby from his arms with a wide grin.

"Come on, Frankie, better come with me in case your daddy's sense of humor is contagious. I'd hate for you to have to go through life with that burden."

## *Chapter Three*

Josh's life was getting a whole new kind of perspective as he walked the streets of Southern California. He'd known he was boring, that his life was routine and stagnant, but now as he passed a transvestite on roller skates he realized how sheltered his life had been. His father had been a dedicated obstetrician for over forty years when he handed his well-established practice off to Josh. It was the passing of a torch that Josh wasn't convinced he even wanted. Sometimes in a small town, you can get lulled into complacency and when someone offers you a complete life all boxed up and ready to take, it can be hard to turn it down. The free tuition, paid by his father and the connections he was able to maximize during his internship proved too hard to pass up. His father did everything for his future and while Josh had always been grateful, he also felt trapped.

It wasn't that he didn't love being a doctor, as a matter of fact, he was sure it was the exact thing he was meant to do. But being a doctor with his own practice in a small town was watching grass grow kind of dull. He'd spent some time doing rotations in the ER in his younger days and that was where he felt truly alive. The night a man came in with a chainsaw lodged in his neck was still the most thrilling seventeen hours of his life. The adrenaline. The accomplishment.

Bringing babies into the world had its own kind of excitement but lately all it seemed to do was remind him how far outside that club he was. Having kids wasn't even on his radar yet, no matter how badly he wanted it to be. Every cute squishy-faced child he wrapped up and tucked into the new parents' arms was a harsh reminder of how empty his life was.

The only spark of heat he'd felt lately was when he was with Willow. Something about her made him feel alive, as vital as he was in the emergency room that day. Maybe it was just the drama she brought with her or the look of need in her eyes when she and Jedda first stepped into his office for help. Maybe it was the edgy way she talked and moved that had him pulsing with excitement. Either way, he knew he needed more of it in his life. He let her stay out here alone, completely unbothered by him, for months. He went back to his routine and the excruciating boredom. But that phone call, that voicemail, had reignited his desire for her.

He looked down again at the address Bobby had written down for him. The phone they were tracing led to an approximate location that led to a lease written under an assumed name, Claudia Talaveriti. With some research, Bobby was able to uncover the fact it was a fake identity with no history. This was where Josh was headed and all he could hope was the girl who left him that voicemail was still someone who wanted his help.

He approached the apartment building that looked like a row of dismal dorms. It was three levels high, all beige and block shaped. Imperial Beach was far different than he imagined. Landing in San Diego, he judged too quickly how nice it might be where Willow was staying. The drive south had opened his eyes. The number of windows with bars on them and the number of houses in disrepair seemed to grow with every passing mile. Now as he drew in a deep breath and readied himself to walk up the cement steps toward the building he thought about what it must be like for her to live here alone.

He paused with his hand on the rusty metal door as a frightening thought hit him. What if she wasn't alone? It wouldn't be so strange to think that after months of being out here, maybe she'd met someone. Maybe that drunk phone call was just that, a drunk mistake. He looked up to the windows above his head and saw the cracked glass and half dismantled fire escape and convinced himself he had to find out.

The three flights of stairs were narrow and dark, each door numbered though most were missing the actual metal numbers and only the dirt that had darkened the door could distinguish where it used to be. As he reached her door, he gave himself one more out. This could be it. He could still turn around and go back home. Back to his unobtrusive office and his quiet apartment. But there was no comfort in those thoughts. Just the opposite really.

He knocked lightly on the door and then listened carefully to hear what type of footsteps might be coming in his direction. Two sets? One? There were none. He knocked again a little louder, but there was still nothing. In any other situation, it wouldn't even cross his mind to turn the knob. But he didn't have a backup plan. He'd rented a car to get here, but hadn't booked a hotel. Finding Willow was his first priority and leaving here without seeing her wasn't an option. To his surprise, the knob turned freely and the door creaked open. Who the hell didn't lock their door in a place like this? he wondered as he stepped in quickly and shut the door behind him.

"Willow?" he said in a hushed voice, not wanting to scare her if she were here. He tiptoed through the small studio apartment and realized quickly that if he couldn't see her, she wasn't here. There would be no place to hide.

The one room apartment left nothing to the imagination. Everything was crammed into a few hundred square feet and Willow hadn't done anything to make the place even marginally comfortable. There was a twin bed, a small kitchenette, a desk and a chair. Her clothes were stacked up on the floor and her guitar propped against the wall. At least he was in the right place. He'd be able to spot her guitar case from anywhere, even though he'd never seen it before. She must have bought it out here. But they'd talked endlessly about music and the case had the stickers of all the bands she loved. It was like her own skin, her own identity right there propped up in the corner of the room. A little tattered but beautiful and full of soul.

He took a quick spin around the room and then his eyes settled on the wall over the desk. He had to move in close to make out what was in front of him. There were pictures of people that had been cut out of photocopies of newspaper articles. There were phone numbers and notes all pinned up together. There were hundreds of tiny slips of papers with one or two lines written on each. A handmade calendar of 1998 with events written in the different squares.

"You're lucky I recognized your cologne," Willow's voice cut in behind him and sent him jumping.

"What the hell?" he barked back as he threw his hand over his racing heart. "You scared the shit out of me. You look so different." He eyed her from her black combat boots up to her even darker hair. He noticed her cheeks flush as she pulled the wig from her head and ran her fingers through her short blond hair.

"How rude of me scaring someone who's broken into my place. If I hadn't known it was you, you'd be dead right now." Willow flashed him a switchblade and then with a frightening level of expertise flipped it closed.

"Your door was unlocked. I didn't break in. Don't you think you should lock your door? It's not like this is the best neighborhood."

"Every place can't be Edenville," Willow snapped back. "Is that what you came all this way for? To give me lessons on home safety? How did you even find me?" Willow tossed down her bag onto her unmade bed and folded her arms defiantly across her chest.

"You called me," Josh said, raising an eyebrow at her, wondering if she even remembered.

"No, I didn't," Willow insisted, but he could tell by the look on her face that she wasn't entirely sure.

"Do you want to listen to the voicemail you left me two days ago? It was pretty unsettling, enough to make me get on a plane and come out here."

With a roll of her eyes, a flare of recognition fell over her face. "I was drunk."

"Yes, you were. But you still called me," Josh said, widening his shoulders and trying to look as unmovable as possible. Hoping to appear too formidable to kick out.

"Did I ask you to come out here? Because I don't even think drunk me would do that."

Josh considered lying. Would she be more willing to accept his presence if she thought in a drunken stupor she'd invited him? As he thought through his decision, she answered for him.

"No, I guess I didn't invite you since you hesitated. So then I appreciate the advice about the door and goodbye." She gestured for him to go but he didn't move. He thought back to Piper's words about not pushing too hard. He'd prepared himself for a much more forceful ejection from her apartment. The fact that she hadn't physically tried to toss him out was a good sign in his opinion.

"Is this it?" Josh asked, as he turned away from her and back toward the wall. "This is what you were talking about in your voicemail? This is Pandora's box?"

"I said that?" Willow asked, sounding like she'd just lost her breath and she wanted to kick her own ass for the comment. She recovered from the show of weakness with a harsh rattlesnake like lunge. "It has nothing to do with you. I shouldn't have called. It was a mistake. It won't happen again. I don't need you here."

As much as those words irritated him, he found a way to look past what she was saying. "I know you don't. I'm not here to try to convince you to go home, or even back to Edenville. I'm not trying to hook up with you or make you fall for me."

"So why are you here?" Willow asked, narrowing her eyes at him.

"Because you called me and that means something to me. I know you don't need me here and you don't need me to help you with whatever you are trying to do, but I'd like to stay." He felt the urge to step forward but he fought it. That is what it would be like with Willow, wanting to go toward her but waiting for her to step forward instead, and never really knowing if she ever would.

"What I'm trying to do is kind of screwed up," Willow said shrugging it off. "And you have your job, you can't just be out here."

Josh was hearing Willow's objections weaken. Even her body language was relaxing at the idea of him staying.

"I have someone covering my patients for me. I'm

my own boss. I can stay out here as long as I want to. As long as you want me to."

"I can do this by myself," she asserted as she stepped by him and sat in the chair by the desk. She was now farther in the apartment then he was, and her sitting down told him she wasn't likely to try to shove him out the door.

"I don't doubt that at all. But since you don't really have to do it alone, wouldn't it make sense to let me give you a hand?"

"I guess," she shrugged again as she started stacking the loose papers on the desk, clearly trying to look distracted.

"So are you going to tell me what exactly all of that is?" Josh asked, pointing up toward the wall littered with notes and pictures.

"Not yet. First, we need to go buy more rum. Otherwise I don't think I'll make it through this conversation."

"So drunk Willow likes talking to me, but sober Willow doesn't?"

"Will it hurt your feelings if I say yes?"

"The only thing that would have hurt my feelings is if you kicked me out. I can deal with you needing to be half in the bag. Judging by your voicemail, you're very poetic when you have a buzz."

"That wasn't a buzz that was practically a coma." She threw her bag over her shoulder and headed for the door. "Lock this on your way out, God knows what kind of crazies will just let themselves in."

## *Chapter Four*

With a bottle of rum in one hand and a bag of takeout in the other, Willow led Josh back up to her apartment. She kept telling her brain to shut up. She begged it to stop feeling relieved to have Josh with her. But she was.

"How much of that do you need to drink before I find out what's going on?" Josh asked as she swigged back another long drag of the spicy booze.

"About this much more," she said drawing an imaginary line on the bottle. "But I can start by telling you why I came to California." She plopped down on her bed and he on the chair by the desk. "I know what you think of me. You think I'm a thief and I run from my problems. You think I stole those drugs for Brad, but that isn't really true. And you think I just bailed on Jedda. You must think I'm scum." Her voice slurred a bit and she knew she was fading into the protective cloud of being drunk.

Though she was sounding miserable, the truth was, when she rounded the corner of her apartment steps and smelled Josh's cologne she hesitated outside the door for a moment and thanked God he was there. The darkness she was falling into frightened even her soul, which had spent its share of days without much light. She thought that eventually someone would come for her. Her adoptive parents or maybe Bobby but the only person she really wanted to see was Josh. And now though she wasn't sure why, she felt obligated to remind him of all the reasons he shouldn't care about her. As though she should wear a warning label.

"You don't get to decide what people think of you. They decide. I know you took money from your parents, but I also believe you probably didn't feel like you had much of a choice. And the thing with Brad, I would have listened to the truth if you would have told me," Josh asserted, ignoring her attempt to bait him or get him to rehash her mistakes.

"I'm telling you about it now," she snapped, shooting up to a sitting position and throwing him a look. Though she was relieved he didn't agree with her assessment of herself. "I did take my father's prescription pad and give it to Brad. Not because I knew he was going to make drugs. He told me he had a buddy who had gotten hurt really bad skiing when he was supposed to be going to class. He didn't want to tell his parents but he needed something for the pain. He gave me this sob story and stupid ole Willow was so desperate to be liked that I fell for it." She took another sip of the rum and thought back to that day. "He used it to fax in prescriptions for medications that could be used to create these boutique drugs he was selling. They're pretty much chemicals all mixed together and packaged all pretty for rich people to buy. But they aren't safe. Obviously, since they put a kid in the hospital and he'll never be the same." She shook her head and looked up at the ceiling as she thought about the boy who is suffering because of these drugs.

"You screwed up, bad judgment, but it's not like you were out mixing up drugs and selling it with him."

"Don't give me that kind of out. I don't deserve it."

"Fine. So what, you came out here, stole the money from your folks and you got Brad arrested. How in the world did you pull that off?"

"How could someone like me, someone so helpless

pull it off? Is that what you're asking?"

"No, I just don't know anyone who could do something like that? I'm not asking because I think you're weak, I'm wondering because if it were me I wouldn't have known where to start. I'm curious."

"I remembered Brad talking about a guy out here. Marcario. He wanted to get in with the guy so badly. Brad had said Marcario had means and access to the border but that he needed what Brad had so it would be perfect. I didn't know what he was talking about but it all made sense once I knew what Brad was involved in. So I found the guy." Willow let her body fall back onto the bed and tossed one of her heavy arms down over her eyes as she continued. "The rest is complicated, but I met with him. Offered him a deal that was mutually beneficial, and just held my breath and hoped he'd take it."

"I don't even know what that means," Josh said half laughing, leaning forward and running his hand through his hair. Looking like she was blowing his mind.

Peeking out from under her arm Willow watched Josh's eyes scanning her. "Don't look at me like—like I'm some kind of freak." She shot back up to a sitting position as she tried to control her defensive tone. "Marcario isn't a bad guy. I mean, he isn't a great guy, but when I met him I realized he wouldn't be easily tricked into being what I needed, which was a fall guy. He was too smart for that." Willow took note of the change in Josh's posture, a jealous bolt seeming to shoot through him. The urge to calm his reaction was something she tried to ignore. If he were jealous, that wasn't up to her to fix. He wanted the truth and she was giving it to him. "But he's still a drug dealer. He cares about money. So I pitched him an option that got rid of his competition and took

Brad down in the process. All made possible by greed."

"Wait," Josh interjected, getting to his feet as though moving around might help her words make sense in his head. "You walked up to a drug dealer with twenty thousand dollars and made a deal with him, and he just took it? Just like that?"

The question was leading, and Willow was smart enough to read between the lines. Josh was asking: Did you have to do anything else to strike this deal? Why was this man so accommodating to you?

"Just like that," Willow shrugged, not wanting to dive into the multifaceted relationship she had with Marcario. Josh, a man from a privileged life and a normal family wouldn't understand what connection she had with Marcario. Damaged people gravitated toward each other. He'd never understand why a man chose a life like Marcario's, no more than he'd understand why Willow would risk her life the way she had. "Like I said, it's complicated. But it's done. Brad's in jail, Marcario's competition is out of the way."

"Yet you aren't finished?" he asked, leaning against the bare, pictureless wall and folding his arms. "When you left me that voicemail, you implied there was more to be done. You'd started something you couldn't stop?"

"How's Jedda doing?" she deflected, biting nervously at her fingernails. "Me leaving, did it make him worse?"

Josh looked as though he wanted to force her back on topic but then talked himself out of it. "He's doing well under the circumstances. I'm impressed with how hard he's working to get his anxiety and PTSD under control. He goes to counseling twice a week and he's managing with meds. The restaurant's done wonders for him too. I can tell he's learning a lot from Clay and Betty. But he's still very worried about you. It took a lot of convincing for him not come out here."

"Is Crystal still there? Did they work their stuff out? I know she lied to him but I've been doing a lot of thinking about that. He has to understand how desperate she was to find her sister. I can't imagine going that long without knowing what had really happened to someone I loved. It's devastating and it just clouded her judgment."

"She's still there, living in an apartment above the restaurant. They seemed to have come to an understanding about it. I think Jedda can relate to the fact that Crystal lost her bearings while looking for answers."

"Crystal is kind of how the wall started," Willow mumbled, not feeling confident in her own words. She rose to her feet and crossed the small cluttered room, stepping up to the twisted collage she'd created. It reminded her of an eighth grade art project where she had to cut pictures out of magazines to show a pattern, but this was much darker than that had turned out.

"How so?" Josh asked, speaking as though he were trying to negotiate with a wild animal, not wanting to spook her, but also pulling her back to him and this moment.

"Seeing Crystal's face that day as she held up her sister's picture and begged me to try to remember, it was powerful. It really rocked me." Willow ran her hand across one of the notes pinned up against the wall as she continued. "I spent a really long time telling my therapists and my adoptive parents and myself that I didn't remember anything from that time in my life. Bobby showing up on Block Island to talk to me about Jedda last year was like a sledgehammer against the glass wall I'd built. The cracks just kept coming. I started letting little memories back in."

"That had to be scary," Josh offered, taking a couple steps toward her.

"That's where all of this came from. I did nothing to help these girls. They were in my parents' house, I knew they didn't want to be there, yet I never told anyone."

"What do you mean? Your real parents were keeping them against their will?" Josh asked, and the horror in his eyes made Willow want to stop speaking. Josh hadn't had this type of awfulness in his life before and she would be the one opening his eyes to it.

"Yes, just like later on, I was chained to the wall, they were there first."

"You can't take that on yourself Willow. You were a child, like six or seven years old. There is no way you could have intervened. You wouldn't have even known what was happening. You couldn't have grasped that." His hand reached out and touched Willow's shoulder, willing her to listen.

"I knew something was wrong. I heard the girls cry and plead to go free. I heard them punished for it." Willow lost her breath for a moment and felt the urge to fall forward into Josh's waiting arms. Instead she steadied herself. The memories of how the girls were treated for crying out, was by far the most haunting.

"You were a prisoner yourself. You were a little girl." Josh insisted, lowering himself slightly to force Willow to meet his eyes.

Willow shook him off and turned back towards the wall of information she'd built. "I wasn't always chained to that wall Josh. That came after. After those girls were chained there first. I was free, walking around, talking to people. Going to school. I could have done something. I'm going to do something now."

"I'm not going to argue with you. I disagree about your level of guilt in the situation but I won't waste my breath. You say you want to do something about it now, what exactly do you mean?" Josh folded his arms across his chest clearly finding it difficult to not reach out and hold Willow.

"I remember three girls. Not everything about them but pieces. I've been writing it down. When I came out here, I just wanted to be open, just cracked open and let all of this out. But I can't remember some things."

"It's very common for someone to block out moments in their lives that were painful."

"But I'm working hard to get them back, all the memories. I know they are there. Like this girl," Willow said, reaching up for a piece of paper covered in her notes. It was the one she'd gotten the furthest on. Her most promising lead. "She was Hispanic. It was Valentine's Day when she showed up at my house. I remember her wearing a shirt that said so. I was six. She was maybe ten or eleven at the time. I wrote down which songs were popular on the radio at the time. What food my parents brought her to eat. I know it's not pertinent but anything I could remember I wrote down here. I can't remember her name, but I can still see her face," Willow whispered as she closed her eyes. The way she uttered the words was as haunting as the memories themselves.

"I'm sure her disappearance would have been thoroughly investigated already. Maybe they already know the link to your parents. You might be carrying this burden for no reason."

"When Jedda killed my parents he did what he

thought was right by pleading guilty and not going to trial. He was trying to protect me and he did. He kept me out of the news and gave me a chance at a normal life. But because of that choice, they never discovered the horrors that were going on in my parents' house. They never heard why Jedda killed them. I never told anyone, and no one ever dug deeper. They were just the people murdered by their kid. I have to do something with this information."

"I agree. But you need an emotionally safe place to try to remember and then you can turn over what you do to the authorities. There are professionals who specialize in helping victims of crimes recover repressed memories. It can be a really slow process, but it's effective and safer than trying to do what you're doing. I have a friend from medical school who went into psychiatry. I can contact her and --

Willow interrupted angrily, "That's not what I want. These girls could still be alive. That happens, they find these girls ten or fifteen years later, still prisoners but alive. That really happens." Willow could see the solemnness spread across Josh's face and she knew he didn't share her hope.

"Ok," he said, nodding his head and biting slightly at his lip, clearly holding back words he'd like to say.

"I want to go back to where I used to live. Back to the neighborhood. Talk to people, read articles and public information about cases and missing girls. That will help me remember. I'll be able to piece this together."

"Don't you think the police could do more with the information than you?" Josh asked, still looking like he was afraid to spook her, but trying to temper her misplaced hope.

"No. I think they'll think I'm crazy. Or they won't take it seriously enough and everything I say will end up in a drawer somewhere collecting dust. I need to put it all together and hand them something they can't ignore."

"Ok," Josh relented, nodding the same way as he had last time he said the word that was starting to infuriate Willow.

"That's it? Just ok? You aren't going to try to talk me out of it? You aren't going to tell me I should go back to Edenville or Block Island?"

"I'm not stupid enough to think there is anything I can say to convince you. And I'm hopeful enough to think you'll let me come with you."

"Why would you do that? You have to go back to work. You can't just run off and help me chase this down."

"Don't worry about my work. It's covered. I have time."

"But you don't think this is a good idea, I can tell."

"Who cares what I think? If you feel like this is what you need to do then I'll help you."

"But you must have an opinion." Willow dug her heels in, needing to hear Josh say the words. She wanted him to admit he thought she was wrong, though she didn't know why it was so important to her.

"I'll be whatever you want me to be right now Willow. You want me to blindly support you? You got it. You want to hear what I think as a doctor? Fine. Or you want me to be a friend? It's your call."

"What would you say if you blindly supported me?"

Josh looked thoughtfully at the ceiling as he searched for the words. "I would tell you that you've got this. You're tough and smart and you can do it. That you're right."

"And as a doctor?"

"As a doctor I'd tell you," Josh swallowed hard before he continued, "I would tell you that it is incredibly dangerous to go into an environment like that and try to stimulate the return of those memories without being under the care of a professional. It can be potentially catastrophic and result in something as serious as a psychotic break. You'd be opening a floodgate and could very easily find yourself swept up in the undertow. The odds of any of these stories having a happy ending are statistically low. If that's the case, it could push you over the edge. You're likely to feel worse, and possibly need significant professional intervention if you try to go it alone."

Willow averted her eyes again, trying to take in his words without letting them scare her. She needed to face this but his advice couldn't be ignored.

"And if you were my friend?" she asked quietly, turning her eyes back toward him. This answer was the one she was most interested in, the one she needed to hear.

"I would tell you that if all of that happens, if it's too much and you can't take it, I've got your back. You won't be alone." The earnestness in his voice was piercing through Willow's armor.

She tipped her head back toward the ceiling hoping gravity would keep the tears that were forming from falling. "I need to do this. I really believe that."

"Then let's book some flights. You say you remember her face? We can find a sketch artist. I think getting it on paper could help." This was his way of showing he was serious, actually willing to help, not trying to trick her into coming home. And it was working.

"That's a great idea," Willow smiled and stepped toward him, not yet sure if she intended to touch him, though she wanted to. "You're really going to do all this with me?"

"Yes. But there are two catches. If you are in mortal danger, I will intervene. I'm not willing to commit to letting you destroy yourself. If it gets to that point, I'll step in. Otherwise, I'll just watch your back and take your lead. Second, I plan to call Edenville. Everyone there is concerned about you and I don't intend to lie to them. You don't need their permission but they love you and you should give them an update."

"Fair enough," she nodded and nervously began wringing her hands together, unsure of what else to do with them. If she didn't keep them busy, she knew they'd reach out and touch Josh's kind eyed face.

"You should know, I'm not here to try to win you over either. I'm not going to kiss you, or make a move on you," he assured seeming to read her mind. "I'm not going to risk having something with you someday just to have something with you right now."

"I don't know what things are going to look like when I come out on the other side of this." She felt obligated to warn him that there might not be anything left of her worth caring about.

"Just don't lose yourself in this. Make sure there is still enough of you left on the other side to piece back together."

"I'll try," she said, pushing her bangs out of her eyes and finally meeting his gaze again. She wouldn't make a promise, but this was as close as she'd get to doing so.

"We can fly out tomorrow if you want to pack up.

I'll grab a hotel and pick you up here in the morning."

"Stay," Willow said, quicker and with more urgency than she would have liked to portray. "I know it's not a really nice place but I want to show you what else I have here," she continued, gesturing up to the wall of information she'd pieced together so far.

"Sure, I can crash on the floor," Josh offered trying to make the situation less awkward.

"The floor is disgusting. If we're really going to do all this, if you've truly got my back and plan to support me, I think we can share a bed. I mean, just like sleep in it."

"That's fine," Josh smiled, clearly amused by the hot pink in Willow's cheeks. "I think I can handle that."

## Chapter Five

Piper held her tongue as long as she could as everyone gave his or her opinions on Josh's phone call. She watched as Michael's nostrils flared the way they did when he was angry. His tone made it clear he was.

"So she did have a hand in what happened to Brad? Does she know how bad it would have been if anyone had found out? That document I sighed was iron clad, she needed to put the Brad stuff behind her," Michael seethed.

"Apparently she had more than just a hand in it. She orchestrated the whole thing. Getting involved with some very dangerous people in order to do so. From what Josh said she's lucky she didn't get herself killed," Bobby huffed as he slid into his booth at the Wise Owl. The restaurant was doing great but Monday nights were always quiet so they made it a point to come, making sure the seats were filled. It was a nice addition to Wednesday night dinner, though Piper could see the conversation might get intense.

"Well if it's done now why doesn't she just come back?" Jules asked, as she patted Frankie gently on the back and pushed her pink pacifier back between her cherry red lips.

Bobby, who'd taken the call from Josh, looked like he was mustering the courage to bring on more bad news.

"I'm starting to get to know that look," Jedda worried out loud, tossing his dishtowel over his shoulder and sitting down to join them. "It gets worse, doesn't it?"

"She's not coming back here," Bobby admitted, and Piper let out a heavy sigh. She didn't think the odds were good that a little time away would get Willow back in a happy state of mind. She knew from experience it took a lot of work and a lot of help. Hiding out didn't do you any favors. "Josh just booked them two flights back to New Jersey. He said she's got this plan in her head. Somewhere along the way, she started remembering things from when she was young. She remembers other girls who came through the house, girls your parents abducted maybe. Her plan is to go back to your old neighborhood, the old house to try to remember more and find out what happened to the girls."

Jedda pinched the bridge of his nose with his fingers as though his head was about to burst from the pressure. "Bobby, you of all people know how dangerous my neighborhood was. It's likely even worse now. She can't go tracking down my parents' old connections and try to find out what they did with girls they abducted. She'll get herself killed. I'm going up there."

"You can't go Jedda," Crystal interjected, a comforting hand squeezing his arm. "She won't let you just drag her back here anyway. She's a tough cookie, she'll put up a hell of a fight."

"I will literally toss her over my shoulder and carry her back here if I need to." Jedda grunted as he pounded his fist on the table sending the silverware rattling.

"Crystal's right," Bobby agreed, sucking in a deep breath. "Jedda can't go there but I can and I don't care what she wants, I'm getting her home. I don't care if I have to handcuff and arrest her. At this point she's done enough to warrant it."

"I recall you just giving Josh the wild horse speech. You're changing your tune now?" Piper asked, finally speaking up. "I thought you were speaking from experience. Do you really think a plan like that would have worked on me?"

"She's not you Piper. You never stole money or drugs. You weren't out associating with guys like Brad or God knows who else in order to take him down. What you were doing was admirable."

"That's what I was doing in Edenville," Piper admitted. "But I had a whole life before turning up here. Trust me, some of my mistakes would make Willow look like a nun."

Bobby threw Piper a curious look as he asserted, "All I'm saying is I think she needs a firm hand at this point. Josh went out there, and I was hoping he'd talk some sense into her. Clearly he didn't."

"She's a grown woman and Josh is with her. If this is what she thinks she needs to do then we should let her," Piper stressed, raising her voice to meet Bobby's volume. They didn't do much arguing these days. Their lives had settled over the last few months, but Willow had remained their one point of contention. Bobby hadn't fully shaken his views of right and wrong and Piper hadn't been able to ignore her empathy for Willow's situation.

"Josh has lived in Edenville his whole life. He's not going to be prepared for what it's like up there. Think about how Jules was when you got to New York," Bobby reminded. Piper knew he expected her to be on his side but she wasn't. She knew what it felt like to be paralyzed by life as though you couldn't move forward until you fixed the things haunting you.

Jules cut in with a stern look, "I did just fine up there, thank you very much."

"You've been going to school for a while now,

Piper," Michael said as Betty came in with a tray of food for everyone. "I'd imagine learning to become a social worker and victims advocate you've seen your share of the horror stories. Hell, you've lived them yourself. The statistics don't lie. The odds that any of these women will be found are miniscule. She's not actually going to have a good outcome from all of this. You have to know that."

Piper kept her tone steely, knowing a lot was riding on this debate. "I'm not saying I think she's going to find them, I'm saying she deserves to look for them if that's what she thinks she needs to do."

"Josh is worried about her mental state," Bobby chimed in now not looking at Piper at all as Betty placed his plate of pasta down in front of him.

"Willow?" Betty asked, putting down the last plate and then taking a seat with all of them.

"Yes, she's going to New Jersey and trying to remember things from when she was younger. She thinks she can help some of the girls her parents hurt. I know it's not likely but I think it's important that she try." Piper pled her case to Betty, knowing if she could win her over, she could turn the tide of this conversation.

Every eye was on Betty, waiting for her to weigh in. She pulled her napkin from the table and placed it on her lap as she thought it over. "Is it safe?" she asked, and her eyes went wide as Bobby, Jedda, and Michael called back a loud and resounding no.

"But she's determined I'm sure?" Betty continued, the wheels in her brain turning.

"She's not going to stop," Piper interjected before anyone else could. "Willow is going to do this, we just have to figure out how to help her, not how to stop her. I'll go up there. I'm off school this month anyway."

49

"You're off school because of your wedding and honeymoon. Don't forget about that," Jules reminded, switching positions and handing a fussing Frankie over to Michael. She took her role as maid of honor very seriously, even if the wedding was planned to be casual.

"You're not going up by yourself. I'll go with you, but I'm not biting my tongue while I'm there. I'm going to tell her this is a bad idea," Bobby said, folding his arms across his chest assertively.

"I'm sure that will go over great. But you don't have any time off, only what you've got scheduled for the honeymoon," Piper said sounding defeated.

"I'll switch it. We'll just honeymoon before our wedding. In Jersey. Doesn't that sound romantic?" Bobby shrugged and leaned into Piper with a sweet smile.

"I'm not sure either of you are capable of relaxing anyway. I figured even on your honeymoon you'd be solving a crime or something," Michael joked, as he grabbed the onions off of Jules's salad with his free hand and Jules grabbed the tomatoes off his. Piper had watched them morph into a couple during the time she'd known them and this was just another example. How wonderful to find the person who willingly gave you your favorite thing off their plate and took away the one thing you didn't like. It brought balance to them both.

"So we're going?" Piper asked, looking around the table in a speak now or forever hold your peace manner.

"I think we have to. I'll give my boss a call and explain the situation. Maybe he'll give me some liberties to work with a precinct up there. If Willow's dead set on doing this at least we can do it the right way."

"If you two aren't here for your wedding," Betty began, pointing her knife threateningly over at them, "I will hunt you down and drag you back here. I have worked too damn hard to make sure you two don't screw things up in this relationship. I'll be damned if I'm going to postpone these vows."

"I think we've done most of the heavy lifting in our relationship," Bobby shot back putting his arm around Piper proudly.

"Oh please, you'd all be nothing without me. Just a bunch of hungry, lonely buffoons who keep screwing up your lives. Let me hear one of you disagree with that and I'll start listing the crap you all pull. So just don't make me get on another plane and pull your sorry butts back here. You know how much I hate to fly." Betty sliced off a bite of meatloaf and plunged her fork assertively into it. "Oh and give my love to Willow. Tell her we're rooting for her and if she needs anything at all, I'm here."

"You're scary and wonderful all at once, Betty," Piper said as she poured a glass of wine for herself.

"You just focus on the scary part if the idea of moving your wedding date creeps into your head," Betty threatened with a sweet smile.

Everyone finished their meals and then began to scatter. Jedda tossed his dishtowel back over his shoulder and tied his apron back on as he kissed Crystal goodbye. Jules and Michael finished the endless process of getting Frankie cleaned up, strapped in, and all of her jingling toys gathered up.

"Piper," Crystal called in a hushed voice once Jedda had disappeared back into the kitchen.

"What's up?" Piper asked reading the look of conflict on her friends face. Crystal had been someone Piper could talk to leading up to the wedding when Jules had been busy tending to Frankie. She'd assimilated well into this patchwork family, becoming her own pattern in their quilt. Crystal was good for Jedda, and in that, good for all of them.

"I wanted to ask you and Bobby something," she said looking uncomfortable as Piper waved Bobby over. "I know this makes absolutely no sense and I'm embarrassed to even ask, but I was hoping you could take something with you when you go to New Jersey." She reached in her bag and pulled out the photograph of her missing sister Erica. The edges tattered and the print faded, Piper could see Crystal had been carrying it a long time. Likely, the entire fifteen years Erica has been missing.

"Of course," Piper answered holding her hand out to receive the picture Crystal clearly didn't want to part with.

"I completely understand that you're going up there for Willow. I'm not asking you to do anything proactively on Erica's case. I know you looked into what was available up there already and there wasn't anything to go on. That hasn't changed. I try not to talk about it too much because I feel terrible for the pretenses I used to meet all of you. Hiding my past from Jedda just hoping he'd have information about my sister that was wrong. But Erica is on my mind every single day. Not knowing what happened to her is the worst part. It would mean a lot to me if you could just take her picture. Just in case." Crystal pressed the photo down into Piper's hand and brushed her long blond bangs away from her eyes. Wiping away a small tear, she bit at her lip.

"It's worth having with us," Bobby assured her as he pulled her in for a hug. There were no shortage of moments in Piper's life that reminded her why she loved

Bobby.

"Thank you both, not just for taking Erica's picture with you but for how accepting you've been over the last few months. I didn't make a very good first impression but somehow you all found a way to give me another chance."

"In this family, we do second chances," Piper smiled, squeezing Crystal's arm. "Hell, we do third and fourth chances too," she teased.

"Well Betty seemed like she meant business so you just make sure you two are back for your wedding. Sounds like you might be out of chances."

## *Chapter Six*

Willow clutched her bag close to her chest as they made their way through the hotel lobby. The notes she'd gathered, the things she'd forced herself to remember were all tucked away in the pockets of that bag and they felt as important to her as oxygen. She didn't want a single scrap to be lost. She couldn't afford to a have a piece of the puzzle misplaced, even if much of it was unimportant.

"You sure you're alright with me only getting us one room?" Josh asked hesitantly as he pushed the elevator button.

"Yeah, I don't know how long I'll be up here and it's too expensive to get two rooms. I think we can be adult about it."

"Absolutely," Josh agreed, grabbing Willow's guitar case and gesturing for her to step into the elevator ahead of him. It was those small acts that, all stacked up together, made Josh who he was. His arm reached out across the opening to ensure the doors didn't prematurely start to close on her. His movements were always accommodating and kind. Selfless. He'd likely let the elevator door chop off his arm if it meant she got in safely. Luckily, it didn't come to that and he stepped in behind her.

"I called the sketch artist. She's going to meet with us here in the lobby tomorrow morning. Is there anything you want to do tonight or did you just want to rest? I'm sure the jet lag is harder on you, adjusting to the time change and all."

"I want to go to the apartment. Even if we don't go

inside, I just want to get there. I need to see it all," Willow said, fidgeting with her nervous hands. Maybe that didn't make sense to Josh, but to her it was a crucial part of what she was doing. She'd splintered off so many pieces of her life that until she saw that structure, the actual building standing there in front of her, she wouldn't be completely convinced any of her memories were real. This was going to set the tone. Would Josh really support her or would he take every opportunity to talk her into backing off? Would he suggest they rest, grab dinner and start fresh in the morning?

"Sounds good. I put the address in the GPS earlier and we're about twenty minutes from there. I wanted to make sure we were close enough to get back and forth easily but that we were staying in a safer area." With those words, Willow felt another of her defenses fall away. He'd passed every test so far, and she was starting to wonder if he really could just support her.

"That's smart. I think it'll be good to have a home base that's far enough away in case I get overwhelmed." Admitting the chance that she might struggle was her gift to him. She wasn't dumb enough to think this wasn't going to take a toll on her, but normally she'd put up a blustery front about how she'd have it under control. Josh deserved to see that she was nervous, that she was being realistic.

"Let's get our bags settled then head out. I don't think we should be there after dark, do you?" Again, Josh wasn't dictating, he was letting it be her choice, her idea.

"Definitely not." Willow smiled as Josh opened the door to the hotel room and she felt a wave of relief flow over her. She'd been living in that decrepit miserable hole for so many months. A nice clean, comfortable bed in a safe place was exactly what she'd hoped for even though she wasn't going to ask for it.

"I know I already said it a bunch of times Josh, but I don't feel like I'm saying it the right way. Maybe I don't even know how. The fact that you're here, the way you're backing me up… it's helping. I think it's going to make all the difference. I know I don't really ever get the words right but…"

"Message received," Josh said with a flash of understanding in his eyes. "I know taking help isn't easy, so I'm just glad you haven't tried to lose me yet."

"Trust me, if I wanted to it wouldn't be a matter of try. I can disappear." Though she meant it more as a joke than a warning, she regretted it as she saw a seriousness fall over Josh's kind face.

"Don't disappear," he pleaded as he pushed his hair off his forehead and stared straight into her. "Just don't."

"I won't," she assured him, even knowing the odds were against that being true.

They settled themselves into the hotel and Willow found herself antsy to leave. Her nervous energy was practically shooting sparks out of her as she paced around the small hotel room.

"Ready to go?" Josh asked as he tucked in his shirt.

"You should change," Willow suggested, trying to be tactful. "You look like a doctor. Did you bring anything else?"

"What's wrong with looking like a doctor?"

"Doctors are rich. Rich people get robbed," Willow explained as she grabbed his bag and set it on the bed, quickly unzipping it. She was finding boundary crossing unavoidable. Last night they'd slept in her lumpy too small bed. Their bodies were forced to touch and they woke in each other's tangled arms. Pawing through his clothes for something better to wear was just another line to cross and it seemed like it would be one of many.

"Here, what about this?" she asked, tossing him the only T-shirt in the bag. "Just leave it untucked."

"Do I look like someone who tucks in his t-shirts? Boy, if so, I need to work on my image."

"I wasn't sure," Willow laughed, and she wondered if she should leave him alone to change. Before she could decide, he was already reaching over his back and lifting his dress shirt over his head, exposing his well-defined chest and stomach. His tanned skin was smooth and begging to be touched.

"Shit," she breathed out before she could catch her words.

"What?" he asked, grabbing the T-shirt.

"Do you work out? I didn't know you had all that under your white coat and stethoscope. You're in really good shape. Like really good."

"So I'm full of surprises today. I'm not the goofy chubby guy who tucks in his T-shirts. I'm glad we're clearing this up."

"I didn't think you were chubby, I just didn't realize you had a damn six pack," Willow retorted as she covered her own midsection self-consciously with her hand. "What's that?" she asked pointing at the long jagged mark that cut across his lower stomach and trailed below the waist of his pants and out of sight. She couldn't help but wonder where it ended.

"It is a scar and someday I'll tell you how I got it. There are a lot of things you don't know about me Willow. But you will."

"I guess if we're going to be in this three hundred

square foot room we'll be finding out a lot about each other."

"I'm looking forward to it." Josh smirked as he opened the door for her. "After you," he said waving her by him.

"Where did you learn to do all that?" she asked, hesitating on her way out and turning her body to face his, the small space of the doorframe forcing them close to each other.

"Opening doors? Well I think they covered operating common door knobs in med school."

"Not the actual opening of the door, but all that stuff you do for people, for me. Holding doors, grabbing my bags, making sure I'm good before you worry about yourself. That has to come from somewhere."

"I don't know really. It just always seemed like the right thing to do. I guess my dad must have done a lot of it and I just picked it up. Then as I got older, I kept doing it because I liked the way it made me feel. Maybe it's the doctor thing, wanting to help people."

"You're like a real gentleman. I don't know that I've met anyone who does that stuff all the time."

"Now you have," Josh retorted, and Willow felt the urge to kiss him. She leaned her face in a few centimeters and felt his hand brush against her shoulder, not seductively but haltingly. "We probably only have a couple hours of sun left, we should head over to the apartment," he said as he leaned back the equal distance that she had leaned in, sending a loud message.

"You're right," Willow conceded, talking more about the fact that he'd rebuffed her kiss than his comment about the daylight fading. He was indeed right, a kiss now could be catastrophic.

# *Chapter Seven*

As Josh's car rounded the corner to the apartment building where she'd spent the first part of her life, Willow felt weirdly excited. She wasn't enthusiastic about remembering the horror that had occurred there, but she knew it was the first step in possibly finding these girls.

"That's it right there." Willow pointed as they approached the four-story apartment building with splintered dark brown wood siding. "Holy shit." She brought her hands up to cover her mouth.

"You okay?" Josh asked, laying his hand on her leg gently.

"It looks exactly the same. Just as shitty. I really remember it. I know it doesn't make any sense but I didn't really believe this was all real until right now."

"I'll park and we can walk around if that's what you want."

Josh pulled into a spot and before he could cut the engine, Willow was swinging the door open and heading for the front of the apartment.

"You have a plan here? I'm with you; I just want to know what you're thinking." Josh explained, trying to keep pace with her.

"I'm not thinking," Willow admitted as she heard Josh trying to catch up. She thought he might grab her arm and try to talk some sense into her but instead, he just met her stride.

"Can I help you with something?" a man in a beige jumpsuit asked as he stepped between them and the door.

The words Willow hadn't taken the time to think

through didn't magically form. She stood with her mouth agape, a look of panic filling her. Josh's voice and his extended hand toward the man were enough to shake her from it.

"I'm Doctor Nelson, this is Willow. We're interested in seeing one of the apartments in this building."

"You must be lost," the man said with a wary tone as he reluctantly shook Josh's hand. "We don't have any doctors living in this building, that's for sure. I've been the super here for twenty-one years, I can tell you this ain't the apartment for you."

"We're not looking to rent it," Josh began to explain but a spark of recognition ignited in the man's face as he cut in.

"I know you," he said, pointing at Willow who immediately turned her eyes toward the ground. "I saw you on the news. You used to live here. The guy who killed his parents, that's your brother right?"

Willow couldn't speak. The last thing she expected to happen within her first five minutes here was to be recognized. She'd mentally separated herself from everything this place represented. It was a stark reminder that this wasn't something she hovered above and watched happen, she'd lived all of this.

"Yes," Josh cut in, stepping forward between the super and Willow slightly. "You were here then?"

"I was, I remember it all. I remember you. You were little. All these years I thought your brother was just a psycho but the news said they let him out."

"He was protecting me," Willow mustered, regaining her voice with a shocking fierceness. "They let him out because he didn't deserve to be in there."

"That's what I heard," the man said with wide eyes

as though he was looking at a ghost. "People were saying your parents were like monsters or something. That they had you tied up in there? If I had known that..." The man's tiny voice trailed off. His face wrenched with guilt.

"It's ok," Willow assured him, not wanting anyone else to carry the remorse she did every day. "They were monsters, but I don't think many people knew."

"Why do you want to see this place again? I would think you'd never want to come back."

"I wasn't the only one," Willow started, the words catching in her throat. "There were others and I want to try to remember. Maybe help them. Find them."

"There were other girls kept up there? The news didn't say anything about that. How did they keep them so quiet? How did we not know?" The man put his hand over his forehead as though his brain was hurting from the shocking news.

"They were pretty good at scaring the girls into being quiet. They had their ways," she gulped out, hoping he wouldn't ask her to elaborate. One of the most terrifying things about talking about her past was the inevitability of someone asking her why she never tried to get away. She could see their faces were filled with the burning question, Why not run? Why not scream? Why not fight? It was hard to explain, even harder to admit.

"That's very brave of you to come back and want to help," the man said, pulling a large ring of keys from his belt loop. "My son lives in the apartment now. It was empty for a long time after. Eventually I rented it to my boy once he was old enough. Come on up. He's at work and won't mind if you look around."

"Thank you." Josh smiled as he looked over at Willow and clearly expected her to be smiling too. That was not the case. The fact that she was moments away from stepping back into a hell she'd convinced herself she'd dreamed up was not something she could smile about. The excitement had waned. Evaporated really.

"No," she said, her legs cemented to the ground. "I can't." Her words felt far away, as if someone else were speaking them.

"It's really not a problem. My son won't mind. He wasn't much older than you were at the time but he knows what happened. He'll understand."

Willow's eyes glazed over with the threat of tears as she locked her gaze with Josh, speaking to him without words.

"I really appreciate your time today. I think she might not be ready to go inside. She needs more time," Josh explained, stepping sideways and using his body to shield Willow from the building. It was a hollow attempt but Willow took the act to heart.

"Here," the man said, fishing in his pocket and pulling a business card out. "You call me. My name is Tony. Anytime you want to see the apartment, I'll let you in."

Josh took the card and flashed a grateful smile. As they turned to head back to the car, Willow looped her arm in his, a necessity to keep from falling. This was the wave Josh had talked about that might bowl her over, and nothing had even happened yet.

"Willow," Tony called pulling their attention back toward the building, "you're tough. You were back then. I remember."

A small sniffle escaped from Willow as she sent back a halfhearted wave.

"I'm sorry," she whispered, taking in a raspy breath.

"I'm sorry I didn't go inside. I just need more time."

"Don't apologize to me," Josh consoled, stopping at the passenger side of the car to let Willow in. "The fact that you didn't go inside right now is a good sign. It means you're not recklessly plunging into this as if it doesn't have repercussions. You have to listen to your heart. You'll know when you're ready and if you never are, that's okay too."

"It's not okay Josh," Willow shouted, pounding her fist into the car. "Those girls might still be out there. I might be the only person who can find them."

"Careful, that's a rental," a voice called out sending Willow's hand shooting to Josh's bicep, her nails digging in.

"Bobby?" she heard Josh say and she tried to focus on the people moving toward them.

"What are you doing here?" Willow demanded with a sharp edge to her voice. Bobby's voice had rattled her and it made her reaction harsher than she meant it.

"Willow, please, let us talk to you," Piper pleaded as she stepped around the car toward them.

"Did you know they were coming?" Willow asked throwing daggers at Josh with her eyes. She wasn't meaning to sound so brash but they'd startled her at a moment when she already felt uneasy.

"I didn't know," Josh answered, tossing his hands up in innocence. "I swear." He looked like he knew the consequences if she didn't believe him.

"We're here to help," Piper tried again, placing her hand on Willow's shoulder.

"I don't need your help. Didn't I make that clear in Edenville?"

"Hold on," Bobby said, his tone firm. "Do you think

it was easy for us to just take off and come up here? Like we don't have lives of our own?"

"No one asked you to!" Willow called back, matching his tone. "I am trying to do something here. Something you wouldn't understand. I don't need you here." Having Josh around was one thing. He'd proven he was willing to quietly support her, but she doubted Bobby and Piper could make the same commitment. They'd never agree with what she was trying to do and they'd likely try to get her to give up. She didn't need that energy around her right now.

"We're not here for you," Piper said, softening her voice and pulling Willow's eyes back to her and away from Bobby. "We're here for Jedda. He's going mad worrying about you. If we didn't come he would have and he can't do that right now. You know that." Piper raised an eyebrow, imploring Willow to agree.

"He is?" she asked, her voice quiet and childlike. "He wanted to come up here? I thought he was still pissed about the way I left."

"He's not pissed. He was ready to pack his bag. He's worried and you know how hard it would be for him to come back here. You know, because you're going through it too. We're here so he doesn't have to be. Can you understand that?" Piper asked, her face soft, her voice lulling Willow into an understanding.

"I guess so, but there isn't anything you can do. There's no point in you being here. You aren't going to convince me to stop this or to go home. I have things to do here."

"I get that," Piper said, trying again to touch Willow's shoulder, to connect. "I've been there. We're not going to force you to do anything but Bobby and I can help. You just have to let us."

The silence between all of them was thick, no one sure where to turn the conversation next. Was Willow's lack of words a sign of agreement? Bobby, whose body language was screaming impatience, was the first to break the quiet.

"Did they not let you in the apartment? I can go talk to the guy you were just with, is he the super of the building? I can always flash my badge."

"Were you guys standing here the whole time?" Willow grunted, feeling like she was an animal at the zoo being watched for fun.

"We just pulled up a minute ago and saw you talking to him. We didn't know you were going to be here. Our plan was to just come check it out before we found you," Piper explained, though it did little to ease Willow's jumping nerves.

"So am I going to talk to that guy or what?" Bobby asked, taking the badge that hung on a chain around his neck out from under his T-shirt.

"No, he's nice," Willow said, averting her eyes. "He'll let us in. I'm just not going in today."

"Why?" Bobby cut back, and Willow saw the look Piper shot to quiet him. A powerful one, reserved only for women who knew a man well.

"What?" Bobby asked in response to the dirty look. "I'm just asking. You're here saying you're on this mission. Well, let's get on with it then."

"It doesn't work like that Bobby," Josh said with a steady seriousness that made her grateful he was in her corner. "She'll do it when she's ready. Today isn't the day. There are other things we can do first. We have other leads."

"Leads?" Bobby asked with an air of annoyance in his voice. "You sound like you're the one simplifying things. You might not like what I have to say while I'm here but I'm the only one who's going to be able to open some doors for you with these leads. I'm here to help, but I don't have that much time to do this so if we're not going in that apartment like you planned then what are we doing?"

Piper rounded on Bobby and planted her hands on his chest, backing him up four or five large steps before whispering something to him. He didn't respond, just nodded his head as they stepped back toward Josh and Willow.

Bobby didn't speak when he rejoined them but the way he was forcefully biting his lip spoke volumes.

"Willow has one girl she remembers the most. I think it could be enough to get a name if we know where to look. Like a missing persons website or something?" Josh offered, settling his voice from combative to neutral.

"Let's go get something to eat," Piper suggested hopefully. "You can tell Bobby and he can maybe help you find out more about her." Without a word, as though saying yes was too committal, Willow shook her head in agreement as Josh pulled open her car door.

"Bobby you grew up close to here, I'm sure you can find a place to eat," Piper said with a smile that didn't match the atmosphere of the group, but it was clear she didn't care. They'd all have their role in this and Piper would be the peacemaker. It was like she was a translator, responsible for standing between Bobby and Willow in order to interpret the conversation for each of them. Her job would be to strip out the tone and the bite of the words and remind each of them the well-meaning and justified intentions of the other. Willow certainly didn't envy that task, but she was glad someone filled the position.

## *Chapter Eight*

To describe the meal they shared as awkward would be an understatement. No matter how much Josh and Piper tried to make it marginally more comfortable, Willow and Bobby kept taking potshots at each other.

So it came as a surprise when they stepped outside the old Italian restaurant and Bobby touched Willow's shoulder lightly. "Walk with me?" he asked her as he gestured down the street. Josh and Piper immediately and with little attempt to make it look natural, turned their backs and began chatting about the weather.

"Sure," Willow shrugged not even pretending to look like she wanted to go.

"I'm sorry you think I'm being an ass," Bobby grumbled, as they headed toward the park across the street.

"You're sorry I think you're being an ass or you're sorry you are being an ass? I've got a different response depending on which one of those you meant."

"You always have a smart ass remark, don't you? You remind me a lot of Jedda when he first moved in with us. I was so excited to have a brother, but he was always shooting his mouth off. Eventually he warmed up to us though," Bobby remembered as they headed toward the deserted playground.

"It has nothing to do with me warming up to you. I don't want anyone around me right now who thinks what I'm doing is stupid or impossible. It's not impossible."

"It's improbable," Bobby started and then bit at his lip, trying to shut himself up. "What Jedda did, it changed all our lives. I'm sorry if I'm being hard on you. It's just

68

that the people around me, they are finally hitting their stride. Jedda's doing well. Jules has her life together. Piper is in a great place. Even I'm over my own crazy ideas of what I thought I could have done to stop Jedda. We're all getting past it and I just wish that you," Bobby stopped short as Willow cut into his words.

"That I'd pretend I was over it too? That I'd just act happy? I've already tried that. It's not working. This isn't about Jedda killing our parents. It's about the people they hurt before he killed them. It's about being silent and staying silent for too long. I'd think as a cop you of all people would want to piece this together."

"That's just it, Willow, I do. I want to take whatever it is you know and hand it over to the cops up here and let them do their jobs. I'm not saying you should bury this and just move on. But there is a difference between sharing what you remember with the authorities and completely immersing yourself back into the darkest time in your life."

"You tell me right now that those cold cases get the attention they deserve. Look me in the eye and tell me that some flashes of memories I have will be taken seriously. Or, like I'm trying to do, I can walk in there with something complete, something they can't ignore. I owe it to these girls, these faces I can't unsee. I want to help them."

"The odds aren't good Willow. Happy endings are not real life. You didn't go in that building today. It was too much for you. So what makes tomorrow any different? I just don't want to see you lose yourself in this. You could stop now, I could help you find the right detective, and you could go back to your life."

"What life? Move back to Block Island so everyone

can treat me like a leper? I'm sure my parents have been crucified over this and I'm the last person they want to see."

"They call me every Sunday," Bobby said as he walked over to the creaking swing set and sat on the blue rubber swing. Willow took the swing next to him and leaned her head against the chain as she closed her eyes.

"They do?"

"Yes, they want you home. They don't care about the money or anything else. They love you."

"They're just saying that now. The reality of me actually being there would be different. I'm never going to unsee this stuff Bobby. I pretended it wasn't there for so long but it came back and now it's just burned into my brain. I can't quiet it. But maybe if I do this, I'll at least have some closure. Making this right, it feels like what I have to do."

"You're the face that's etched into my brain," Bobby whispered, kicking some mulch mindlessly with his foot as he rocked a little in the swing. "The day I followed Jedda and walked into that apartment it changed me. I've never been the same. You were there all cut up and starved half to death. Chained to a wall like an animal. It's what I see on my darkest days."

"I'm sorry my imprisonment popped the perfect bubble you were living in," Willow snapped feeling defensive. Why that was always her knee jerk reaction, she wasn't sure. But talking about this made her angry, and the closest people to her would have to suffer the backlash.

"That's not what I mean," Bobby corrected. "I guess when I'm here giving you a hard time about diving back into all this, it's because I remember what it felt like that day to see you hurting. I remember how broken you were. I never want to see you like that again. I didn't know you, but I knew Jedda. He was my brother too and I loved him. His heart exploded at the sight of you like that. It wrecked me. I don't want to see him go through that again either."

"Bobby," Willow huffed as she slowly parted her eyes, letting the light back in, "if I don't do this I will be lost. If there is any hope for me at all it's going to be because I make one small piece of this right." It went against every ounce of her nature but she tried to muster the right words that would let him know she could hear what he was saying without acquiescing to what he was asking. "I need to do this, but I'd like your help." And with that, the hunch in his back and the tilt of his exhausted head disappeared. Straightening like an arrow his words came quickly. That was Bobby's Achilles heel, a friend in need.

"I'll help you. Piper and I will both help you. If you really feel like this is your only way to get through this then we'll do it together. Just promise me something."

"I don't think I can make any promises right now."

Bobby ignored that excuse as he spoke. "No matter what happens, however this turns out, you'll come to our wedding in two weeks. Jedda needs you there."

"I promise to try," Willow conceded, as she pushed off and began to swing with impressive speed.

"I haven't done this in years." Bobby chuckled as he got his bearings on the squeaking swing. "Well if you don't count the porch swing."

"It's weird how different it is. Don't you think?" Willow asked pushing off forcefully with her feet.

"How so?"

"When I was a kid, I'd swing until my legs ached. All I wanted to do was go so high my feet hit a cloud. Now my stomach sinks the second my feet leave the ground."

"The older you get, the more you see in the world, the more fragile everything feels. It's like you know better than to try to touch the clouds because you might fall. You miss out on soaring through the sky."

"That's depressing," Willow groaned, as she pumped her legs to gain more speed.

"That's adulthood," Bobby shot back with a shrug of his shoulders as he stepped himself back and then launched his body toward the sky on the swing. "But we can always try to fight it." He laughed as he pumped his legs and aimed for the clouds.

## Chapter Nine

"That's a pretty big pile of notes," Piper remarked as she took a seat next to Bobby and across from Willow and Josh. The hotel room was too small, a restaurant not private enough, so they'd taken refuge in the empty study room in the back of the city library.

"Some of it is just gibberish," Willow shrugged as she spread the haphazard papers out in front of her, proof she wasn't any sort of private detective. As Bobby reached across the table to take the sketch Willow had assisted in making that morning with the sketch artist, she snatched it away. "I wrote down everything I remembered. Even things that don't make any sense, just in case they do at some point. Some of these are descriptions of the men I remember coming to the house. They might be involved. I know it looks like a random stack of nonsense, but it's in an order that makes sense to me, so don't touch it."

"Sorry," he said raising his hands and eyebrows all at once. "Where do you want to start?"

"There are three girls total who I remember but I want to start with the one I know most about and hope more comes back to me about the others as we go." She slid the sketch along the wood table toward Piper and Bobby but never took her fingers off the paper, indicating they could look but not touch. "This girl is Hispanic. I heard her speaking Spanish to herself a lot. Praying I think. She was around ten or twelve years old and showed up in 1998 on Valentine's Day at my house. She never told me her name but," Willow paused trying to make this all as clinical as possible, leaving emotion out of it, "she mentioned a baby brother. I think she called him Carlitto. I don't remember how long she was with us. I don't know where she went, though I do recall multiple men coming in to look at her. But I wasn't there the day she was taken, or bought or whatever. That's all I know."

"That's a lot," Josh reassured her as he looked over to Bobby clearly hoping he'd do the same.

"It is," Bobby agreed. "The date, the age, the sketch. All of that will help. We should be able to use missing persons records to get a name. Then we can see the status of the case."

"What do you mean the status of it? You think they would have found her? I'm sure whoever took her would have disappeared with her. That's why I think we need to track whomever the men were who bought her from my parents. We need to know how they contacted them and how their entire operation worked. I want to find the scumbags who paid my parents to steal kids for them."

"Isn't all this about helping the girls?" Piper asked, getting the question out before Bobby could, and giving it a lighter spin than he likely would have.

"It is. I think that would be the quickest way, don't you?"

"No," Bobby said flatly. "Whatever your parents did, whoever they worked with, too many years have gone by to dissect that. We're talking about vagrant and transient people who are accustomed to doing business in an underground way. There isn't going to be a paper trail. The girls--getting their names, understanding when and how they were abducted--that's the stronger lead. So let's go with it," Bobby used a definitive tone as he opened his laptop. "My captain has given me a pretty long leash. He said as long as I don't piss anyone off I can work with the precinct up here and tell them I'm investigating some cold cases with leads that turned up in our jurisdiction. It's not entirely true but I'll tread lightly."

"Fine," Willow grumbled as she slouched back in her chair with a huff. "We'll start there."

"The information you provided will actually do well in the missing persons database. I'll plug it in and see if anything meets those parameters," Bobby said as Piper leaned in close to him. "It's kind of a one man job." He smiled and playfully shrugged her away.

"How long does it take?" Josh asked, and Willow could tell her nerves were rubbing off on him.

"It's coming up now." Bobby grabbed a pen and paper to jot down the results. "There are four girls who were reported missing on Valentines Day in 1998." The pause in his voice brought everyone leaning in a few inches closer with a look of impatience pulling at the corners of their faces. "None of them match the description you provided. A two-year-old, a seventeen-year-old, and two five-year olds are coming up. The cases were all closed within a couple days, which usually means the kids were found quickly. I'm looking at the pictures and none look anything like the sketch."

"That can't be right. I know for sure she came to our house on Valentine's Day." Willow's voice was shaking with disappointment.

"Could she have been somewhere else for a few days? Maybe you can expand the search?" Josh asked, resting his hand on Willow's forearm to try to calm her.

"The wider you cast the net the more fish you have to go through to find the right one. I'll put the age range and physical description in, too, and see if we can narrow it down." Bobby tapped harder on his keys as though he was willing it to give him something. "I went back six months. There are nineteen girls matching that description and in that general age range but none look very close to your sketch." He spun the computer around so Willow could take a look for herself.

Her eyes scanned the screen, scrutinizing the features of every girl. With a squint of her eye and a slight tilt of her head, she prayed she'd see her. But she wasn't there. "This doesn't make sense. Something is wrong with the database. Are you doing it wrong?"

"I'm not doing it wrong," Bobby snapped back momentarily losing his composure. "Maybe she was taken much earlier and held somewhere else. Let me see if I can change the parameter."

"She wasn't," Willow said forcefully spinning the laptop around. "She was crying for her parents like she'd just been taken from them. She cried for her mom every day. She still had the terrified look in her eye, not the hardened dead look that comes later. She was taken on Valentine's Day or shortly before." The bite in Willow's words mixed with the painful sharp edges of her memories was enough to quiet the room.

They all looked back and forth between each other as they tried to figure out how the girl might not have ended up in the missing persons database at the time Willow knew her to be missing.

"Wait," Bobby said as his fingers moved fiercely across the keyboard. "Here she is." He spun the computer around again and pulled the sketch from under Willow's hand, holding it up next to the screen.

"Yes," Willow shouted and then quickly covered her mouth with her hand partially because her voice had been too loud for a library and partially because she knew she was about to cry. Her chin quivered as she leaned in and stared at the photograph of the girl she had failed. The girl she knew was in trouble but did nothing to help.

"Do you need a break?" Josh asked his hand sliding up to her shoulder and squeezing it tightly.

"No," she said, shaking him off. "What does it say? How did you find her? When was she taken?"

"This doesn't tell me when she was taken, it tells me when she was reported missing. It dawned on me that sometimes parents wait to report their kids missing if they aren't expecting them home for some reason. So I expanded the search to the end of February."

"Smart." Piper smiled rubbing Bobby's arm, a proud look on her face.

"There's a problem though. She wasn't reported until two weeks after Valentine's Day. Her mother filed the report."

"Why would a parent wait that long?" Josh asked, his eyebrows furrowed in confusion. "That doesn't make any sense."

When Bobby didn't answer, Piper's face fell with a sad realization. "She wasn't abducted, she was acquired. The parents were in on it?"

"They both have a history of drug arrests. They were addicted to meth." Bobby scrolled further down the report. "It's possible that for a price they turned their daughter over to your parents and delayed filing the report as a means to make sure the trail was harder to follow."

"What?" Willow asked breathlessly. "They gave her up, like a used car they just traded her for money so they could score drugs?" She pounded her fist down on the table. "Then we find them too. We track them down."

Danielle Stewart

Somewhere in her mind, Willow had built a fantasy that involved finding this girl and reuniting her with the family she'd been ripped away from. The slicing open and gutting of that possibility was painful.

"They're dead," Bobby said pointblank. "The mother overdosed, the father was killed in a prison fight. We can't know for sure if they sold her or if she was abducted but it would explain the timeline issue."

This wasn't at all what Willow was constructing in her mind. She'd imagined these girls riding down the street on their pink bikes with white streamers flowing from the handlebars and her horrible parents pulling them away to a terrifying new reality. She hadn't prepared herself for so many others to be culpable. There were too many bad guys in this scenario for her to wrap her mind around.

"What's her name?" Josh asked in a calm voice, pulling Willow back into a hopeful place. He didn't say, what was her name. He didn't make her existence past tense.

"Josephine Vasquez. She was eleven years old when reported missing. The actual case file, not the missing persons report, has been marked as closed. I don't have access to it, but if I go down to the precinct and they are open to the idea I should be able to see where it stands."

"Why would they close it, because they found her?" Willow asked, a dim flash of hope jolting through her.

"Yes, if they hadn't found her the case would be marked cold or open. So if it's closed it means they've located her or her body." Bobby's voice trailed off and though it was clear, he wasn't trying to, his words shot through Willow like an arrow.

"So being closed means she might be dead?" Willow

78

asked a vulnerable tremble in her voice.

"Or that she was found safe," Josh added, though it was apparent he was treading lightly. And for good reason. Bubbly optimism was just the kind of thing that would send Willow running for the hills at this point.

"It could be either," Bobby admitted as he scratched down more notes in his book. "Do you want to go over what you remember about the other girls now or do you want me to go chase this?"

"She," Willow hesitated, "Josephine is the one I remember most clearly. I think we should get this answer first. I'm going to go back to the apartment today. I know going in there will help me remember the others."

"You sure you're up for that?" Piper asked and Willow ignored the pins and needles all over her body as she nodded her head "yes."

"What about tracking down your parents things?" Bobby asked as he closed the computer. "Some stuff would have been entered into evidence by the crime investigator who processed their murder. But mostly everything else would have been deemed nonessential and was likely left behind. Maybe if you don't get into the apartment today for whatever reason, you can start looking for their belongings."

"We can call Tony back. He's the super of the building and has been for a couple decades. If anyone knows what happened to their things it would be him," Josh said with a hopefulness in his voice.

"You guys call us if you find anything out, and we'll do the same," Piper said as she and Bobby headed out of the room.

"How are you feeling?" Josh asked in a hushed voice. "You did so great. I mean she has a name now.

That's incredible."

"I feel like shit," Willow snapped standing and slinging her bag over her shoulder. "I didn't want to find other deadbeat parents. I didn't want to think that no one even wanted her."

"You don't know for sure that was the case. It's a theory. You're remembering a lot of your time in the house now. I can tell. What's that like?"

"Are you being a doctor right now?" Willow asked, halting in the doorway and forcing Josh to stop quickly, and bump into her slightly.

"I'm just asking."

"It's awful. Sometimes I feel like I was just a fly on the wall. I feel like I'm looking down on myself, watching it all play out. But sometimes it all feels very real and I remember I was really there."

"But you aren't anymore," Josh said, brushing her short blond hair away from her downturned eyes. "This is all moving really fast Willow. I know that Piper and Bobby are on a time crunch and I don't think they understand what this is putting you through. Maybe we should have them back off?"

"No, I want this moving fast. It's like a Band-Aid; I just want to yank it off so I can start to heal. I want to find Josephine. Bobby is my best chance at that. We don't have to be getting along perfectly for us to still get this done. I can manage how I'm feeling."

"Okay," Josh said, shrugging. It was clear to Willow that he wanted to press her to keep talking about this, but he just nodded and continued. "I'll call Tony and we can head over to the apartment."

"I'm going in this time," Willow said with a glare in her eyes that flamed with resolve.

"Then so will I."

## Chapter Ten

"I think you're being a jerk," Piper called over her shoulder to Bobby as she hailed a cab and considered getting in without him.

"A jerk?" he said incredulously, hopping in beside her and nudging her firmly with his hip as Piper gave the driver the address to the police precinct. "She's the one with the bad attitude. I reached out to her last night after dinner but today she's all snippy with me again."

"She has every reason to be a mess right now. You need to support her. Take a couple on the chin and soften your approach with her. She doesn't need a grumpy big brother figure telling her how she feels is dumb."

"Well what does she need?" Bobby asked, his tone no softer than it had been all day. "She's out there thinking she can play detective. Did you see that pile of notes? She's in for a rude awakening when these cases turn out to be messier than she thinks. Whatever she's dreamed up in her mind about the outcome is highly unlikely. It's not going to turn out how she wants."

"Exactly," Piper sniped as she checked her phone for messages.

"What do you mean exactly? What is that telling me?"

"Figure that out Bobby and I think you'll finally get it. I swear, for a sweet and smart guy sometimes you're a dumb jackass."

"I love you too, honey," he grumbled playfully. "Do me a favor, when we get to the precinct please let me do all the charming. Judging by this conversation, your skills are rusty."

"I'm right about this Bobby. Stop going hard at her. She doesn't need it." She slipped her hand into his and they laced their fingers together. "I'm glad you're my dumb jackass," she whispered as she rested her head on his shoulder.

"I couldn't think of any other pain in the ass I'd want calling me names," Bobby replied, kissing the top of her head.

As the cab pulled up to the police department Bobby fished his badge and notebook out of his pocket. They passed through the front doors and stepped up to the wooden booth with a window in it. Through a static filled microphone, the cop on the other side scrutinized Bobby's credentials and his authority to be there. After thirty-five minutes and four phone calls, they finally let them in.

"Hello Officer Wright, Miss Anderson, I'm Detective Denny Styles. I head the cold case task force. We get lots of families in here begging us to look into something or other, but it's not often I get a cop in here saying he might have leads for me. You've piqued my interest."

"Thank you for meeting with us right away Detective Styles," Piper said with a smile as they walked down the long and painfully bland hallway toward the back of the office. She took note of his out of date mustache and mustard pinstripe yellow shirt, his pocket lined with pens. He looked like the kind of man who was more at ease in a dingy quiet office digging through a mountain of paperwork than having to deal with people.

"Please call me Denny, and don't thank me yet. What I'm sure Officer Wright will tell you the second I leave is the only reason they've assigned me to help is to determine if you really have new leads on cold cases. If you do, it will be my intention to steal said case and information from you in order to further the success of my department. I'm less of a liaison and more of a double agent."

"But admirably honest." Bobby grinned. "Call me Bobby, and trust me, we're fine if you take point on the case. I'm on a limited timetable here and I'm just happy to have some help. That's if there is a case at all. I've gotten a tip from a close friend of mine and I want to see it through. This first one I'm bringing you doesn't seem very promising, but maybe one of the others will pan out."

Denny showed them into a small room and flipped the overhead lights on, sending the bulbs instantly into a hum. "You have a friend with information on multiple cold cases? Are you sure he didn't commit them?" Denny laughed, his wide smile lifting his large ears up almost an inch.

"She was seven years old, I think it's safe to say she wasn't involved." Piper retorted curtly and she knew she was being too sensitive. The cops she'd gotten to know through Bobby, all had a crass sense of humor at times. It was an obvious coping mechanism for processing the horrors they saw on a weekly basis.

"Here's the case file number," Bobby said, taking a seat across from Denny and sliding the notebook to him. "This morning the girl worked with a sketch artist to come up with a rendition of the missing person she remembered. Then I searched the missing persons database with the information she could recall and we got a strong match. My friend ID'd the picture I showed her."

"Josephine Vasquez," Denny muttered as he scrolled

through the case file on the computer screen in front of him. "It's not a cold case, it's closed. She's dead." The disappointment in his voice wasn't rooted in mourning the loss of a girl, but the loss of a chance at being a hero in a cold case.

"That's so sad. How did she die?" Piper asked, trying to quietly guide the man back to his humanity.

"Killed herself," he replied flatly, Piper's attempt clearly unsuccessful. "The missing persons case was filed by her mother. She was assumed a run away. Josephine resurfaces in 2006 when she's arrested for possession of narcotics and prostitution. That's what closed the missing persons case, but she continued to acquire a long record after that."

"We think she may have been originally taken to be sold into some kind of sex trafficking. Is there a chance the prostitution was against her will?" Bobby asked, scratching down all the information Denny was offering.

"Could be. There aren't many ways to distinguish something like that until places get raided and the conditions the girls are living in come to light. I worked on a team a few years back that focused on prostitution. The girls in that area, where Josephine was picked up a few times, run without a pimp. Plus she was arrested six more times for the same charge over the following year and a half. She was put into a mandatory drug center. If she was being held against her will and forced into prostitution that may have been a good opportunity to break free. She went back out a few weeks later and got arrested in an area about seven miles from the corners she was working before. In my experience, this sounds like a profession of choice."

"You say it like that takes away from the fact that

85

she's dead. Like it matters less. She was missing for eight years. Aren't you interested in who took her, where that time in her life went?" Piper was pacing around the room as she felt her anger build. Going to school for victims advocacy had been a cathartic but sometimes traumatic experience for her over the last few months. She knew it was what she wanted to do. She could feel it in her bones. But the stories, all the horrific stories she heard on a weekly basis, were enough to make her want to scoop up all the hurt and exploited children and save them.

"I'm not saying she's worth any less because she was a hooker, I'm saying she's dead and there isn't anything we can do to change that. There's no case here." Denny crossed his arms behind his head and leaned back in his chair.

"You said suicide? Is it solid?" Bobby asked shooting Piper a look that said he understood her point but it wasn't going to help them to keep pushing it.

"Looks like it. She OD'd on pills. Left a note and made a few phone calls to girls she worked the corners with. Notes here say she was troubled. The other girls weren't surprised when they heard." Denny scrolled through more pages of documents as he whistled a cheery tune that didn't match the somberness of the situation. "Nothing in here about where she was for that missing time. She never filed any complaint against anyone for imprisonment or kidnapping. Maybe your friend, she was only seven at the time, maybe she got it wrong. Maybe Josephine wasn't sold. She might have just been a runaway who stayed off the radar for a while."

"My friend's parents were possibly the ones who took her and brokered the deal to get her sold into trafficking. It was their M.O. and she's certain this girl was there against her will."

"If that's the case, there is another scenario that might make sense. These girls, the ones who go in real young, they cater to a certain market of men who desire that age. Josephine may have become obsolete in those circles as she got older. Sometimes they kill the girls, sometimes they get them hooked on dope and toss them out on the street, banking on the fact that they're too damaged to be taken seriously or too scared to ever go after the people who hurt them. There's a lot of brainwashing done to these girls."

"Here's the information on my friend's parents. They're deceased, but we believe they might have been very active in the sex trafficking world. There are other girls. Maybe they're alive, or their cases still open." Bobby slid more papers over to Denny.

"If this really isn't a competition for who closes these cases, then I'd like to talk to this girl. I'm willing to put in the manpower and resources if she can link her parents to an open or unsolved case. But I'm not going to drag this out. Call her up, let's do this today."

"It's difficult," Piper said, finally taking a seat next to Bobby and calming her jittery legs. "Willow's been through a lot. She's fragile. We were letting her ease into the memories. She doesn't even know the outcome of Josephine's story yet. That's going to crush her."

"I don't know what to tell you. If you want the support of this department and its resources, then bring her in today." Denny's face lacked any empathy as he grabbed a toothpick from his pocket and stuck it between his teeth.

"I'll call her," Bobby said finally giving in. "But remember she's a victim too. I don't want to push her over the edge."

"You really think you have some viable leads? We're talking fifteen years ago, these girls are all likely gone in one way or another."

"I know," Bobby admitted as he ran his hand over his stubble-covered cheek. "I'm just not sure she knows that, no matter how many times I've told her."

"I'll leave you two alone and you give her a call. The sooner you can get her in here the sooner we can move forward. It sounds like this might be more about closure for her than anything else. You understand that we just don't have the resources to help her with that."

Bobby and Piper were silent after Denny left the room. Bobby stared down at his phone for almost a full minute before he spoke. "I get it," he said quietly. "They are likely all going to pan out this way, but knowing that isn't going to stop Willow. Nothing I say is going to change her mind. Any of the girls she remembers are probably going to have a similar story."

"Probably," Piper breathed out, squeezing down on Bobby's thigh, reminding him she was still there for him even if he was being an idiot.

"So me sitting there telling her this is how it's going to turn out isn't helping. Being right doesn't really matter," he muttered, the realization clearly not sitting well with him.

"That ship has sailed, she's already out there. You need to decide who you're going to be when it starts to sink."

"I get it," Bobby said again shaking his head. "I'm not sure who she needs me to be. I want to warn her and protect her. It was different with you. Even with Jedda, it felt different than this. Why is it so hard for me to just support her?"

"She's not very likeable," Piper admitted with a half-smile. "But sometimes when people are acting their worst it's when they need love the most."

"You're starting to sound like Betty again," Bobby chided with a grin as he took her hand in his.

"Not even close. If Betty had heard you acting like this, she'd have slapped you upside the head by now. I let it go on longer than she would have. I just don't want to see you be the bad guy when Willow goes looking for one. You have to let her do this."

"It's counter-intuitive. Watching someone you care about do something you know will end badly. Standing by while they walk off the edge of the cliff."

"It's her cliff. Her life might be waiting for her after the drop."

"She's going to come here and find out what happened to Josephine. It's going to knock her down."

"And we'll pick her up."

Danielle Stewart

## *Chapter Eleven*

"No," Willow said, crossing her arms over her chest, her lip clamped tight between her teeth. She'd gotten the phone call from Bobby and listened to the news he'd given her but she didn't believe it. "That doesn't make any sense." It wasn't as if Willow hadn't prepared herself for the chance that Josephine might be dead, she knew that could be the reason the case was closed. What she hadn't considered was that the girl would have been so broken she'd take her own life.

"Where are you going?" Josh called quickening his pace to try to catch her. "They want us to head down to the precinct."

"I can't take this bullshit anymore. I don't care what you say Josh, I know you think this is crazy and pointless. You're humoring me, but if I told you right now I was done, you'd be relieved. You'd tell me I was doing the right thing by letting all this go. You want me to get on a plane and go back to Edenville and act like everything is fine. That's all anyone wants from me, to be fine. To act fine." Willow pulled hard on the handle of a parked cab and threw herself in, slamming the door before Josh could respond. As he hurried to catch her, the cab sped off. She didn't bother looking back to see his reaction. She didn't care. Or at least she was going to force herself not to.

"I want to go to a bar," she said leaning forward and flashing the driver a twenty. "Something in the city, something off the beaten path." The driver grabbed the twenty and grunted as he headed away from the hotel. Willow switched off her phone and pulled the battery out

90

of the back, not wanting to be tracked. She'd heard all of Bobby's words about Josephine but she wasn't letting them sink in. If she didn't acknowledge the truth maybe it wouldn't hurt.

When he and Piper called, it had taken Willow off guard. Tony had just called back to tell them he'd be able to open up the apartment sometime around seven that night when his son went out. When Josh had asked about her parents belongings Tony let him know there were boxes in the basement storage unit of theirs but they'd long since been buried by years of clutter from other tenants. It would a huge job to dig them out.

They'd headed back to the hotel and for a little while. Willow felt a vulnerability that felt welcomed and scary all at once as she sat across from Josh in the lobby. They'd made a promise to not talk about what Willow was trying to do, how she felt, or what she wanted. Instead, they talked about music. It was something that connected them on a cellular level, a language that permeated their souls. It made her think of Marcario. It made her long for a chance to sing in front of his bar again, to see him smile. Not because she loved him, but because there, in disguise she felt so much more protected than she did sitting here with Josh. He made her feel raw and exposed. He'd seen her stripped back and vulnerable. It was a cold and naked feeling that she couldn't seem to turn off in his presence. Maybe that's why after Bobby broke the news about Josephine it felt easier to run.

As the driver pulled the cab in front of the small box-shaped bar with peeling siding and a half lit sign Willow felt herself on a new mission. Drink. Grab a bottle and keep pouring until the sting wore off, until the sharp edges of her memory grew fuzzy. Drink until the anger evaporated. "Thanks," she called out to the driver as she slammed the door and he sped off.

Pulling open the heavy door, she stepped inside and was hit with a wall of cigarette smoke, something she thought was banned in bars, but no one seemed to give a shit. Those were the kind of people she was hoping to be around right now. The ten or twelve bar stools were mostly empty, only a couple of heavy set guys hunched over the bar struggling to keep their faces out of their half empty glasses. A few other men sat in the corner at a table chatting quietly.

No one looked at her, not even the stocky, balding bartender as she took a few more steps in and grabbed a stool at the far side of the bar. When he finally looked up and slugged over, he scanned her with bored eyes. "You old enough to drink kid?" he asked, his hand stretched out for her ID. She pulled it from her bag and slapped it down.

"I'll take a rum and coke, heavy on the rum. And keep them coming."

"I don't want to be picking your skinny ass up off my bar floor in an hour," he growled, raising a skeptical eyebrow at her.

"Just bring me the damn drink," Willow bit back slamming her hand angrily down on the counter. "I'm not a fucking child."

"Whatever," the bartender muttered with a shrug as every head in the bar turned her way. A moment later he was sliding a drink to her and she could feel the alcohol working its magic by the time she hit the bottom of the first glass. By the third one, she could barely feel the ache in her chest anymore. She pulled the pieces of her phone from her bag and fumbled them back into place. There was a phone call she needed to make.

She pulled up the wrong number ten times before finally getting it right. Narrowing her eyes to see the screen of her phone she hit the button to connect the call and let the courage the booze had created take over.

"Hello?" a singsong voice rang out, and Willow gritted her teeth at the happy tone.

"You are so full of shit," she fumed, trying unsuccessfully to hold back the slur in her voice.

"Excuse me?" she heard come back over the receiver, but she didn't let that slow her down.

"You heard me, Betty. You think you have everyone figured out. I can see right through you. It's an act. Throwing weddings people don't even want. Giving advice people don't ask for. It's bullshit."

"Willow dear, I think you're drunk. Where is Josh, or Bobby and Piper for that matter?"

"Probably in a room somewhere wondering how they're going to convince me I'm self-destructive and I need to be stopped."

"If you're alone and drunk right now I might not disagree with them. Can you tell me if you're somewhere safe?"

"Stop it," Willow demanded, resting her head on the cold wood of the bar. "Please stop being that way. I'm calling your bluff. You think you have an answer for everything but you can't solve my problems."

"I always like a challenge. Let's hear your problem and I'll see if my bullshit skills hold up."

Willow let out a breathy laugh. She was expecting to be hung up on by now. She was shooting venom-filled cannon balls and Betty was acting like they were beach balls on a sunny day. "You know what I'm doing up here?"

"Yes I do."

"Of course you do, you know everything," Willow huffed. "I saw these girls. I may not have known everything but I knew they were in trouble and I didn't do anything."

"I suppose you've already heard that you were a little girl and it wasn't up to you to do anything, so I'll skip that."

"Thanks." Willow pulled in another long sip of her drink as she tried to find the right words. The words she didn't want to say. "She's dead. One of the girls, her name was Josephine and she killed herself a few years ago. I don't know what happened to her after she left my parents' house. I don't know how she found herself on the road she was on, but she was so ruined by it all that she didn't want to live anymore." A tear rolled down Willows cheek, though her voice stayed steady.

"That's awful," Betty whispered, but she offered nothing else.

"Damn right that's awful. I knew she might be dead. I'm not stupid. But I didn't think it would be like that. If she got out, why didn't she get all the way out? I don't get it."

"Sometimes all you know, even if it's bad, is easier than starting over. You don't ever have to understand it. It doesn't make sense."

"Now what?" Willow had backed off the insults. She was too drunk, her world spinning too fast to even come up with ways to lash out. She just wanted the answers. That was why she called. There was a small chance that Betty really could make this all better and she needed to find out.

"You want my advice?" Betty asked, not taking the road she could with a tone of indignation, but genuinely asking.

"I think you're going to tell me what everyone else is telling me. I think you're not going to help me. They don't get it, and I don't think you do either."

"I'll take a crack at it honey, and let's just hope if I'm right you're not so drunk you can't remember my wisdom when you sleep this off."

"I'm fine," Willow slurred. "I want to hear what you think I should do."

"You saw these girls, and while you and I may disagree on how liable you are for their situation, I think we can agree that you owe it to them to keep looking until every avenue is explored. You owe that to them," Betty said firmly.

"I do?" Willow asked, an air of surprise in her voice. "I do," she said again, this time as a declaration.

"This girl, she took the path she did. You and I may never understand it. We certainly can't change it. Who knows about the next girl. Maybe she's out there waiting for a person like you to start looking for her. Or maybe she's met a similar fate as Josephine. You won't know unless you finish what you started."

"I don't know how," Willow admitted, her voice small and childlike now.

"Lucky for you I have more bullshit advice to give. Push away whatever bottle you're drowning yourself in and pull your head out of your ass. Go find the people who are trying to help you and get back on track. This journey might break your heart over and over again Willow, but it doesn't mean you shouldn't do it."

Danielle Stewart

"It is breaking my heart," Willow cried as she pushed the glass away from her.

"There's a secret about a broken heart that no one ever talks about. It's not quite as irreparable as people might want you to believe. With the right people around you, it can heal faster than you think. You just have to give them a chance."

"I," Willow lifted her hand to her spinning head. "I just wanted to sorry, I mean say sorry. I didn't mean…"

"Save your sorrys for a time and place when you need them. That ain't now and it ain't with me. I've seen enough in my life to tell the difference between mean and sad. You can call me anytime and tell me I'm full of shit. I'll just sit on the other end of the phone and wait for you to get to the part where you tell me what you need."

"Betty," Willow faltered, trying to make sense of how she was getting let off the hook so easily. "How did you get this way? Were you just born, all–Betty like?"

"I know it's hard to believe, but I spent more years being Willow like. I just woke up one day and decided it was exhausting being mad all the time. It's easier to send love out into the world, because most of the time that's what comes back to you."

"I'm all done drinking now," Willow promised, pressing the phone between her shoulder and ear as she fished her money out of her back pocket.

"Sit your tiny butt right where you are and call Josh. Don't go hopping in a cab and wandering around. You need to make better choices if you're going to get anything done up there. It's bigger than just you, Willow. I think if you focus on that the heartache will be a little more bearable."

"I'll call him," Willow sighed as she rested herself

96

back against the bar.

"And I'll call him to make sure you called him," Betty laughed. "Willow, my door is always open to you. I know here isn't where you want to be today, but if it's ever where you want to be again, don't waste time asking permission."

"Yes, ma'am," Willow said as she hung up the phone, unable to fight the smile. Pulling up Josh's number she tried to focus in on a stationary object, but her grip on the here and now was fading.

"Willow, where are you?" Josh asked with an urgency that reminded Willow how badly she'd screwed up.

"A bar, somewhere not far from my parents' apartment. Hey maybe they drank here. I think it's called, hey what's this shithole called?" Willow shouted to the bartender and she heard some laughter erupt behind her. The other drunks were finding her amusing. "He says it's called, Go to Hell. I don't think that's right."

"Focus," Josh said firmly and it shook Willow from her daze for a moment.

"I'll go outside and look at the sign." She raised her voice to further piss off the bartender. "It's only half lit but that's what you get for coming to a dive."

"Get the hell out, bitch," the bartender thundered pointing at the door.

"Willow, what the hell are you doing? Stop pissing people off. You're alone and you're drunk. Just read me the damn sign and then shut up and sit down outside. You're staying on the phone with me until I get there."

"It's called," Willow tried to focus her eyes as her legs buckled and swayed beneath her, "Liverpool Tavern. That's a stupid name. Oh, hi," she said to the tall dark haired man who stepped out behind her. His skin was marked with acne and his eyes beady and black.

"Hi who? Who are you talking to?" Josh demanded and Willow could hear the mix of fear and anger in his voice.

"What's your name?" she asked the man. "My friend wants to know who you are, but I don't know why."

"Because if he robs or kills you, I'd like to have something to give to the police," Josh said, and though it was worded like a joke, he didn't deliver it that way.

"He just wants to be able to tip off the cop if you rob or kill me."

"I'm not going to do either of those things," the man said in his gravelly voice as he leaned himself against the wall and she did the same. "I just wanted to say hi and see if you wanted a ride."

"Tell him no," Josh shouted so loud Willow had to pull the phone away from her ear.

"I've got a ride coming," Willow smiled and closed her eyes, giving in to the warm lull of her buzz.

"But I think you and I could have some fun. Why don't you hang up the phone and come with me. I'm parked around back."

"Put him on the fucking phone, Willow," Josh ordered, and it was the first time she'd heard him really swear. "I'm going to be there in two minutes and he better not be there when I pull up. Tell him to fuck off."

"He said--"

"I could hear him. I'm not scared. Come on, hang up, and come with me," the man said, tugging at Willow's arm and throwing her off balance. She twisted down and found herself on her ass. "I think I'll stay here," she said, still grinning, the danger swept up and lost in the fog she was in.

The man grabbed her two hands and pulled her back to her feet, which were still too unsteady to hold her up. She took two small steps back and then one large one forward, her face planting into the stranger's chest. His excessive use of body spray was apparent even to her drunken senses.

"Now we're talking baby," the stranger said as he lowered his face to her ear and began whispering as he backed her up to the wall. She felt her back slam harder than it should have as the squeal of tires came tearing up the road.

"Get off me," she roared, shoving the man backward, though he barely moved. There were very few things she remembered from the six weeks of self-defense she'd taken before leaving for school, but a good old kick to the groin seemed appropriate in this moment. She bent her leg and sent it sailing, a direct hit. He bent in half and grunted as he stumbled backward enough for Willow to side step him. She slid herself against the wall a few feet until her body collided with something. It was Josh, and the force of his body on hers was a welcomed crash.

"Bitch," the man shouted as he cupped his groin and inched his way back toward the door of the bar.

"She's a bitch?" Josh asked charging forward. "What the hell kind of guy sees a girl that drunk and tries to make a move on her? You're a bitch." Willow watched in disbelief as Josh clenched his fist and slammed it into the man's jaw. The bartender stepped out just as the blue lights of a cruiser came plowing around the corner and Josh threw a second punch.

Within thirty seconds, both Willow and Josh were face first against the wall their heads turned, so they could see each other as the cuffs were slapped on to their wrists.

"That was so hot," Willow slurred as she grinned widely at Josh.

"Are you okay?" he asked through a grunt as the cop snapped the cuffs on tighter.

"I am now," she whispered, their eyes locked together. "Thanks for showing up."

"If you keep calling, I'll keep showing up."

It was another twenty minutes of sitting on the sidewalk in handcuffs before the cavalry arrived. "I appreciate the call," Bobby said as he shook the officer's hand and looked past him to Josh and Willow.

"No problem. They say you're working some cases up here and they're friends of yours. I normally wouldn't give a shit, but I mean, the guy's a doctor with no record and he says the girl was in some kind of trouble. I figure if you can vouch for them I'll write this up as a drunken disorderly and just give them warning."

"I can assure you, if he was throwing punches it was for a reason. I've known him half my life. He's not a troublemaker. If you could let this slide it would be great."

"Will do, but the girl, she's in rough shape. She needs to sleep it off somewhere."

"I'll get her out of here."

"Are you really working cases up here?" the officer asked as he adjusted his belt over his large stomach.

"I've got some leads on some missing persons that might be linked. My captain gave me some time to chase them down, but nothing's panned out yet."

"Good luck. People go missing here every week. We solve one and three more pop up," the officer said, throwing a quick salute as he headed back to his patrol car.

"You guys all right?" Bobby asked in a hushed voice as Josh stood and helped Willow to her feet.

"She's wasted but I got to her before anything happened."

"Throwing punches huh?" Bobby asked with a smile that showed a glimmer of pride as he uncuffed them both.

"Just because I don't go around kicking people's asses every day doesn't mean I can't," Josh boasted as he slung Willows arm over his shoulder.

"Don't you want to lecture me?" Willow asked, narrowing her eyes at Bobby, feeling a desire to argue with him.

"I'm just glad you're okay," he replied taking her other arm over his shoulder. "We all need to get wasted every now and then."

"I must be really drunk. No one's acting right." Willow rested her head on Josh's shoulder as they headed toward his car. "Josh is punching dudes, Bobby's giving out free passes. What's Piper doing, baking a cake somewhere?"

"Hell would freeze over if that was happening," Bobby laughed as he helped lower Willow into the front seat. "You all set?" he asked, shaking Josh's hand.

"We can give you a lift back, you don't need to take a cab."

"That's okay. She might feel like talking." Bobby slapped Josh's shoulder as he headed for the street to hail a cab.

"I do feel like talking," Willow said as Josh hopped into the front seat.

"About what?" Josh asked, not seeming to have high

hopes for a productive conversation with a drunk person.

"I'm sorry."

"For what, running off, getting drunk?"

"I'm just sorry. I'm tired."

"You can close your eyes," Josh said as he reached over her, his body nearly covering hers as he grabbed her seatbelt and pulled it across her.

"No, I mean I'm tired of being this way. Fighting. I'm just swimming upstream all the time." She moved her hands like a swimming fish and then flopped them down in her lap. "I'll try to be better, you deserve better."

"It's not about what I deserve Willow, it's what you deserve. Whatever you're going to do, do it for yourself."

"Do you still like me?"

"I don't think we should talk about this while you're drunk."

"Stop thinking like the doctor, think like the guy who just knocked that dude's head off," Willow joked, tossing a few sloppy punches into the air in front of her.

"I still like you, Willow."

"I seem like a lot of trouble."

"You are."

"You're not going to kiss me tonight are you? I want you to. But I have a feeling you'll think it's a bad idea."

"That's a good guess."

"I called Betty."

"You did?"

"Yup." She hit the button to put the window down and reached her arm out to catch the wind. "I told her she was full of shit."

"That must have gone over well."

"It did. She ignored that part and just listened to what I was really asking. It made me realize something."

"What's that?"

"I think that's what you're doing. Are you ignoring all the bad parts of me? I think that would be bad for you."

"I see them. I see the flaws. But I'm smart enough to realize they are what you project, not who you are. It's who you want everyone to think you are. I don't think you're as tough as you let on."

"That's funny."

"Why?"

"Because I think you're tougher than you let on. You totally laid that guy out."

"So we're both deceiving. But I think as long as we can see the truth in each other we'll be okay. It doesn't matter what the world thinks of us."

"Will you tell me the secret behind that scar now?" Willow begged, turning toward him with a pleading puppy dog look in her eye."

"I suppose now that you've seen me knock a guy out you can find out about my scar. I was driving home one night and I saw this man getting jumped. I hopped out of my car and fought off six men with my bare hands. One guy had a knife and he cut me before I could knock him unconscious," Josh said animatedly.

"Really?" Willow's eyes were wide and her mouth agape as she pictured the scene in her head.

"No, of course not. When I was ten, my appendix burst and I got an infection. They botched the surgery and I ended up with a huge scar. That's what you get from me Willow. No exciting stories, just normal stuff."

"I wish I hadn't had so much to drink."

"Do you want me pull over, do you feel sick? Please don't puke in the rental."

"No, I wish I didn't drink so much because I would have really liked for you to kiss me tonight."

"I would have like that too."

"Betty says this whole thing of me digging up my past might break my heart."

"It might."

"But that the right people can help fix it."

"I believe that. Do you?"

"I don't know what I believe right now. I know I want to keep trying to do this, to find these girls. That's all I know."

"Then that's what we'll do."

"You might be the best person I know Josh. Even if you think you're ordinary and boring. You aren't," Willow murmured slipping her hand into his. She felt the hesitation in his grip, but that passed quickly and soon his hold on her was firm.

"You know a lot of great people who care about you. I'm just one."

"But you're the best one," Willow whispered as she closed her eyes and her head dipped, nodding off into the sleep that had been calling out to her. Tomorrow was going to be a fresh start and she was going to do just as Betty had instructed, get her head out of her ass and get back to it.

## *Chapter Twelve*

The following morning, in the haze of a hangover Willow sat in the passenger seat of Josh's car as he drove to the police precinct. She'd barely spoken that morning and while she was trying to make it look like it was her way of being introspective, the truth was she was trying not to vomit.

They were escorted into a small room in the back of the precinct where Bobby and Piper were already sitting, looking concerned and impatient.

Willow didn't let the dust settle before she was trying to make her point. "I'm not convinced Josephine was doing what you said. Who would escape one horrible thing and then go right into something else?" Willow had a splitting headache and even though Betty's words had resonated with her, she still felt fighting mad about the details. This was why she didn't want to come to the cops. She didn't feel like they'd put in the work. They'd just write these girls off. She wasn't going to let that happen. As Betty had said, she owed it to them to find out more. That was outweighing her efforts to be kind to Bobby. There was just something about him that made her want to fight. Though she didn't want to admit it she was starting to realize it was because he was usually right, which made her wrong.

"Denny has a lot of experience with sex trafficking cases as well as prostitution busts. He believes Josephine was out there working the streets by choice. Maybe it didn't start that way, but in the end, she was there on her own free will. I'm sorry." Bobby got to his feet, gestured for her to take his chair and leaned against the wall of the

Danielle Stewart

small office.

"How can you be sorry? You were right," Willow snapped as she glared at Bobby. It was easier to be mad at Bobby than to admit the reality of the situation was as bleak as it was.

"I'm not trying to be right. I wish the news was different. Denny is going to come back in here to talk to you soon. He's going to help." It was clear from the strain on his face that Bobby was trying to refrain from snapping back at Willow. It was starting to make her feel guilty for turning him into her punching bag. But she couldn't help herself.

"At least you have more people in your corner, Willow. Having a detective who focuses on cold cases in this area will be a huge help," Josh said, attempting to break the tension.

A light knock on the door interrupted Willows rebuttal and she was grateful for it. "Hello everyone," the musty smelling detective said as he stepped in the room, a notebook in his hand. "I'm Denny." And just like that Willow formed an opinion of him. He was older, probably close to retirement age and that meant he was likely just skating by. He wasn't going to put in the hard work or go the extra mile.

"Hey Denny," Josh greeted him, extending his hand and introducing himself. "We appreciate the time you're taking today. I'm sure you're a busy guy."

"I thought we'd have you in here yesterday but I heard you two were busy in a bar brawl or something. And unfortunately, yes, I'm busy. There is no shortage of cold and unsolved cases here. But that's also why I'm anxious to speak with you, Willow." Denny settled in the seat across from her at the table and put on a warm and inviting smile. "It sounded like you were planning on chipping away at this stuff, all the things you remember. I'm going to help expedite that."

"Why?" Willow asked, rolling her eyes as she took a seat. It was the mix of her hangover and skepticism that was creating the cocktail of bitchiness she was serving. She was afraid if she turned it off, if she stopped fighting so hard no one would listen to her. "You just want to rush through this and get me out of your hair?"

"I don't know if you noticed, but after twenty years on this job I don't have much hair left." He snorted out a laugh at his own joke. "And honestly," Denny continued, pursing his lips together, and shifting to a more serious tone, "I don't have time to have you guys coming in here every day for the next month asking me to check something out. Josephine's case is closed. I can't spend time or resources on stuff like that. I'd like to determine if you have anything useful and then act on it."

"The information I gave you about Josephine wasn't useful? My parents possibly took her. They sold her. You didn't know that before yesterday."

"I understand," Denny replied disarmingly. "Let's just move on to the next case and we can talk about Josephine later."

"Fine," Willow shrugged pulling her notes from her bag and ignoring the throbbing pain in her head.

"First, though, I'd like to know your goal here Willow? What do you want to happen?"

"Isn't it obvious?" Willow replied sharply. Why was everyone being such a dick to her about this stuff, she wondered. "I want to find them. They can't all be dead. I want you to do police work and find them."

"Okay," Denny nodded, though Willow found the

gesture hollow, an obvious effort to appease her. "Tell me about the next girl you remember."

"She came after Josephine. I don't know what month, but it was but it was the same year. Summer, I guess. It was hot and we didn't have an air conditioner. I remember that. Her first name was Liz, that's all she told me." Willow's eyes became glassed over as she let herself remember the whimper in the girl's constant cry. She drifted for a moment and Josh's voice called her back.

"Was she the same age as Josephine?" he asked, clearing his throat as he spoke.

"No," Willow shook her head. "She was closer to my age at the time. Maybe eight. She was white, brown hair, brown eyes."

"That's good Willow," Denny assured her as he turned toward an outdated computer in the corner of the room. "Do you remember anything else?"

"My mom wasn't happy with her. Something was wrong. I think she was sick. My mom kept yelling at my dad about getting a sick one." Willow blinked back a tear as she turned her eyes to the only empty corner of the room. She could feel everyone staring at her and she was afraid to connect with anyone in this painful moment.

"There are a couple girls here matching the description and time frame. Can you look at these pictures?" Denny asked, adjusting the computer monitor so she could see it. There it was again, for the second time in just two days. The haunting realization that her nightmares were real despite years of trying to convince herself they weren't. The face of a girl she tried to forget was staring back at her.

"The one in the middle, that's her." Willow said

quietly, pointing at the screen with one hand and wiping a rogue tear with the other. She felt Josh's steady hand come down on her shaking shoulder.

"Elizabeth Club," Denny said, pulling up her file on the computer. "Her case is closed as well."

Everyone in the room seemed to hold their breath conservatively optimistic that maybe this could have a happy ending. Perhaps the case closed because she was saved somehow.

Judging by Denny's tone it wasn't likely. "She was reported abducted from her front yard in Westville Heights on September seventh. Found dead in a dumpster two weeks later." Denny continued scanning the file as an audible sigh of sadness rolled through the room.

"My parents might have killed her," Willow suggested in a hushed voice that grew as she spoke. "I remember she was there one morning, looking kind of sickly and then gone that night."

"They arrested a man for the crime. He's in prison. Apparently she was diabetic and because it wasn't treated properly, she slipped into a coma and died. He dumped the body and it was traced back to him through forensics."

"But she was at my house. I can attest to that. My parents abducted her and sold her to this man. That's important."

"It's information regarding the case, but I don't know that it changes anything. You can't put dead people on trial," Denny said, twisting his eyebrows up in confusion as though Willow was asking for something ridiculous. "This case is closed. Elizabeth's parents were notified and positively identified their daughter's body. The man who dumped her was convicted and imprisoned.

If your parents were a link in the chain that matters, but it doesn't change what's waiting at the end of it. A dead kid."

"This is bullshit," Willow huffed as she stood and then regretted the sudden movement that rocked her hung-over body. She was just so damn furious, and while she knew no one in this room was to blame, she couldn't wrangle the beast that kept lashing out at everyone.

"Calm down," Bobby insisted, strategically placing his body between her and the door. "I know this is frustrating, but we can't change the facts."

"There's one more, right?" Denny asked, gesturing back to the chair. "You remember one more girl?"

"This is like a morbid lottery. Let's buy another scratch ticket and hope it's not a bust," Willow snarled, as she fell heavily back into the chair. "I don't even know if this is enough. I remember the least about the last girl. She came after Christmas, but I think it was before New Year's. I think she was in her late teens. Her hair was dyed pitch black, with purple streaks. I'd never seen anything like it before. She had on dark, thick eyeliner and messy tattoos scrolled up her arms." Willow couldn't turn toward Bobby or Piper in this moment. She wasn't sure if the spark of recognition lit in them at this description. It was a lot like what Willow looked like when they met her on Block Island earlier that year. She'd been channeling her past and this girl's physical description had bubbled to the surface.

"The date will narrow it down quite a bit," Denny said, rubbing at his temples and rolling a kink out of his neck as he began to type in his search.

"I didn't think it would be like this," Willow quaked showing her first real glimmer of any emotion besides anger. She picked nervously at her cuticles and chipping nail polish as she braced herself for more. "I figured this would take longer. I expected it to be more of a..." she trailed off and Piper cut in.

"A journey?"

"A pain in the ass," Willow grunted, regaining her angry footing. "I didn't think it was possible to find them so quickly." Realistically, Willow understood she needed more time to process this. Having it come together all at once was too much. She was hoping everyone could read between the lines since she didn't have the courage to admit it.

"I've got eleven hits," Denny reported after a few moments, scrolling through the information. "The database has come a long way over the years. Having the timeframe is the best way to narrow down the results. That coupled with the physical description gets us this." Denny turned the computer monitor again and Willow braced herself as though the walls were tumbling in.

"That one," Willow said confidently, amazed that all three faces that had haunted her dreams now had names. "That's her," she reiterated, the unforgettable eyes rimmed in black eyeliner were unmistakable.

Denny quickly turned the computer back toward him and keyed in more information. "This case is closed too," Denny hummed as he typed feverishly. "But the good news is she's alive. Her name is Cleo Swan. She was listed as a runaway, not abducted."

"Where is she now?" Josh asked straightening his back as though everything hinged on this being good news.

"Jail. She was arrested for attempted murder. Looks like she robbed a convenience store a couple years back and fired some shots in the vicinity of the clerk. No one was hurt but she was handed down a harsh sentence. She'll be in there at least another ten years."

"I don't understand how she went from being chained up and sold to running around robbing and shooting at people. What happens from point A to point B?" Piper asked, her brows furrowed in frustration.

"It happens. These girls become obsolete in the trafficking industry when they hit a certain age. It's all they know and many choose to stay in the life in one way or another," Denny explained. "All I know is this is another closed case."

"So that's it," Willow stammered, feeling like the world was caving in on her. "You're not interested in connecting the dots? My parents were criminals. They took girls. They kept them. They sold them. You're not even trying to dig into that."

"Willow," Bobby empathized in a gentle voice that was lost on her, "Denny's doing his job. His job is to investigate open and unsolved cases. Nothing we've brought him so far falls in that category."

"While I was out bouncing from one foster house to the next I'm sure there were more girls. I'm positive they'd been doing this for years. Think about how many cases that might be. The girls can't all be dead or in prison. But you're not even going to look any further." Willow slammed her hand down on the metal table in front of her and refused to let the tears form in her eyes. That would undermine her argument.

"You can't put dead people on trial," Denny thundered out again. "You're brother already doled out your parents' punishment and, in my humble opinion, he got it right. These girls, they don't have family waiting around for closure. There is nothing else to do for them. Could we fill in some blanks in a timeline? Sure. What does that get us? Nothing."

"It could lead to other cases, other girls," Piper interjected, and Willow felt relieved to have a supporter.

"It could, but I already have a room full of case files with active missing persons, murders, and various other crimes. My department has six detectives and over two hundred cold cases. We can't use our resources to go look for other cold cases that might not even exist. If you link any other girls to your parents, we'll explore the information and if it connects to an open case I can assure you you'll have the full gamut of my department's resources. Other than that, I can't offer you any manpower." The finality in Denny's expression lightened a bit as he continued. "However, the department has a very good counselor on staff that would be happy to meet with you. I think it could be beneficial for you to talk to someone about your experience. It sounds like you could use some closure."

"This isn't about me," Willow boomed back as she practically jumped to her feet. "I'm not doing this so I can feel better. It's about you doing police work and chasing down the people who left this damage in their wake. But I can tell I'm not going to get anywhere with you. You're looking for slam-dunk cases. You want everything dropped in your lap. This is a joke." Willow stormed through the door and slammed it tight behind her. A deep down buried sliver of her knew her anger was misplaced. Denny wasn't a bad cop. Everything he was explaining made logical sense, but it wasn't logic fueling her legs to storm out. It was grief and anger and confusion. For Willow, those things mixed together could send her into hyper speed.

"Willow, wait up," Josh called and she could hear Bobby and Piper chatting behind her too. These people were relentless and she couldn't decide if that was a blessing or a curse.

"I know you're pissed," Bobby started, stepping in front of her and halting her with his body. "Those weren't the answers you were looking for. All of us were hoping for a better outcome."

"Really? It sounded a lot like you were hoping this was how it would turn out so you could get back to Edenville." Willow shoved by Bobby and stepped out the precinct door, still feeling everyone on her heels.

"Willow," Josh called again, his patience sounding thin. "Where do you want to go? Let's get out of here and go wherever."

She wanted to tell him to go to hell. To stop being so nice to her when she was being such a bitch, but instead, all she could say was "Okay."

He looked stunned that she was going without a fight but the hole in her heart was so deep she was afraid if she went off on her own it would swallow her up. Going with Josh was the only thing that felt marginally right in a world where everything was wrong.

She felt his hand on the small of her back as he led her to his car and it felt like a tether, keeping her attached to reality. "I just want to go," she said softly as he opened her car door and she sank into her seat.

"I've got you," Josh whispered and ran his thumb across her flushed cheek. As she watched him walk around the front of the car, she cursed and thanked him all at once in her mind. Damn him for being so good to her. It was such a painfully obvious contrast to how badly she was treating everyone.

## *Chapter Thirteen*

"How did you find this place?" Willow asked, sprawling across the hood of the car and leaning her head against the windshield. The engine beneath her was still hot. As the sun was setting and the breeze picking up, she welcomed the heat against her skin.

"I couldn't sleep the other night and went out for a drive. I passed this place and it seemed really peaceful." The tall swaying trees that lined the clearing were a welcomed contrast to the rigid steel buildings of the city.

"I don't really want to talk about it, Josh. Any of it."

"Good, you'd ruin how quiet it is out here," he joked as he hopped up on the hood and lay down next to her.

"Shut up," she groaned as she slapped at his side, letting her hand rest there for a moment as she remembered what he looked like without his shirt on. "So what should we do if we're not going to talk?" She knew the question was leading.

"You could sing. I haven't heard you sing at all since we've been here. Normally you're at least humming something."

"I haven't felt like singing since I left California. When I was out there I was singing almost every night in this bar. Most of the people weren't paying attention, but there were  some who made me feel like they loved it."

"You accomplished something pretty impressive out there. I may not be comfortable with the risks you took but the result was amazing. And you did that on your own. You should feel good about that. Brad is somewhere he can't lay a hand on anyone again and get away with it."

"I guess. I wasn't really alone. I had a friend,"

Willow admitted, turning on her side toward him. Her eyes traced the profile of his face as he stared up at the sky. She slid her hand over his chest and rested it on his heart, the thumping against her palm grounding her.

"I'm glad. I kept thinking of you out there alone."

"Marcario really helped me." Willow closed her eyes and pictured his face. "Being his friend makes me hopeful for us."

"For me and you?" Josh asked, still staring up at the sky.

"Yes, because he wasn't perfect. Not by a long shot. He did a lot of things I didn't agree with or understand but I could still see the good in him. It was like murky water, but if you strained your eyes you could see something shiny at the bottom. I'm hoping you can see the same thing in me."

"I can," Josh assured as he brushed a bit of hair away from her eyes. "I don't have to look too hard to see it."

Too exhausted to fight it, tears filled her eyes and spilled down onto her cheeks. "I don't want to be me anymore," she whispered.

He placed his hand over hers where it rested on his chest and she soaked in the warmth of it. "You can change anything you want about yourself anytime Willow. Just don't change too much. There are lots of parts I like."

"I know that I push people away. I know I'm rude. I'm just so damn angry and confused. It's like I'm waiting for this one big thing to change it all. It wasn't getting Brad arrested. It wasn't finding out what happened to these girls. What else is there?"

"I don't know," Josh admitted, intertwining their fingers and keeping them planted on his chest.

"You're supposed to be the smart doctor. You don't have the answers?"

"This week, all the information and the stories, it's opened my eyes to everything I've been missing, and not in a good way. I feel like I've had my head buried in the sand my whole life. Sex trafficking. Suicide. Dumping bodies. I've been living in Edenville and pretending the whole world wasn't falling to shit all around me. So no, I don't have any advice. This is all new territory for me. Who am I to tell you how to deal with it?"

"That's what I needed to hear," Willow smiled, grateful for the acknowledgement that there was no easy answer. She slid the rest of her body on top of him in one seductive move, and when he opened his mouth in what she assumed would be protest or rational thoughts, she covered his lips with hers. His conflict was palpable, even in the hungry yet reluctant way he was returning the kiss. When her hand slid to his belt, he finally pulled his lips away.

"I know this feels right at the moment, but I don't think−"

"I think we should not think. Just for tonight," she murmured as she pressed her lips to his ear.

"I'm not looking for just tonight," he uttered, but she could tell he was giving in as his hands slipped up the back of her shirt, caressing the smooth skin of her back.

"I know. But it's all I have to give right now." She ran her hands through his hair as she pulled back and stared down into his face. "Can it be enough? Please?"

He didn't answer with any words, but the flicker in his eye was enough. She knew that even the smartest man would struggle to be wise in a moment like this. Leaning back to a sitting position on top of him she slipped her shirt over her head and drew in a deep breath as the sun fell behind the tree line. Josh's hands grasped her hips and the tightness of his grip spoke volumes. She leaned back down to him, pressing herself against the heat of his body and breathing in his musky scent.

Josh opened his mouth to speak and, fearful he'd say something completely logical and spoil the moment, Willow kissed him. She pushed her tongue into his mouth and when she felt his hand tangle up in her hair, she knew he'd have nothing left to say. Words were pointless, reasoning futile; it was time to feel good. Time to feel connected. They didn't have a plan for the future, they didn't seem to be on the same page about much, but right now they were two trains barreling in the same direction and that was enough.

## *Chapter Fourteen*

Making love on the hood of a rental car in a quiet clearing in the woods was perfect medicine for Willow, but it wasn't curative. Waking up the next morning curled in Josh's arms in the hotel room she felt a knot pulling tighter in her stomach. She was awake for nearly an hour before Josh stirred but she didn't move. She was torn between the lulling comfort of being in his arms and the guilt she felt for putting him in this position. Truthfully, she didn't feel any more ready to be with him today than she did the day before, or the day before that. So why did she sleep with him, knowing his heart was on the line?

There'd been no discussion of what today would bring. It was a strategic oversight on her part not to plan past the sunrise but now it was time to face it and she felt terrible for what she'd done. Making love to him felt so perfect but she still felt so imperfect.

"Good morning," Josh groaned as he stretched his body from his toes to the tips of his fingers and his eyes cracked open. "Have you been up long?" he asked sounding concerned.

"No," she lied rolling away from him and on to her back. "I just got up." She pulled the sheet tighter to her body and it made the inches between them seem like miles. She wondered to herself, if you hurt someone, was it better to do it all at once or drag it out? Would leading Josh to believe she was ready for this for another day, or week or month be better for him than just bolting now?

"You all right?" Josh asked as he scrutinized the concern painted all over her face.

"I'm fine," she replied unconvincingly as she slipped

out of the bed and headed for the shower. "I'm sure Bobby and Piper have been blowing up our phones. You might as well tell them to head back to Edenville. I don't need them for anything else." She turned the knobs on the shower. Oddly, she felt like if she sounded unlikable maybe it wouldn't hurt so bad when she told Josh they didn't have a future.

"I figured we should meet up with them. I'll send them a text and maybe we can do breakfast," Josh suggested, and Willow could hear the uneasiness in his voice.

"Fine," Willow sighed as she stepped into the hot water, letting it melt away the pain in her heart for a moment. Josh didn't come in to join her and she assumed her shitty attitude this morning had done the job. She wouldn't say she regretted last night. Not from her perspective. Josh had proved a skilled and perfectly attentive lover. He was the ideal mix of passion and pleasure. She just wasn't looking at it as a jumping off point for the future. It was an event, an isolated event, and she knew that would hurt him.

The rest of the time getting ready was fairly quiet, as was the ride over to the diner to meet Piper and Bobby.

"Good morning." Piper smiled as Willow and Josh slid into the booth.

Willow nodded back and directed her attention immediately to the menu, though she wasn't really hungry.

"Do you feel any better this morning? Sometimes a good night's sleep can really help clear the mind." Piper voice was full of cheery hopefulness.

"I feel fine." Willow shrugged. "I'm just going to eat breakfast and then go back and crash at the hotel."

"We're looking at flights to book back to Edenville," Bobby said taking a swig of his orange juice. "The wedding is coming up fast so we need to get back."

The silence was speaking volumes, no one wanting to ask if Willow was coming back with them. Why wouldn't she? She'd found out what had happened to the girls she remembered. Things seemed to be progressing with Josh.

"You guys must be excited," Josh said, trying to force a smile. "Where are you going for your honeymoon?"

Both Bobby and Piper hesitated before they finally smiled at each other and Bobby spoke. "We're honeymooning here."

"You're coming back up here?" Willow asked, ready to tell them that was the stupidest thing she'd ever heard.

"This is our honeymoon," Piper explained. "Bobby couldn't get anymore time off from work so he took the time he was going to take after the wedding to come up here. It was well worth it though."

"How do you figure that?" Willow shot back feeling instantly like shit for causing them to take something so special and waste it on a useless attempt at helping her. Not to mention she'd treated them like garbage through most of it.

"We wanted to be here for you and now we want you to be there for us. We want you to come to the wedding. Jedda is looking forward to seeing you. We can even have your parents come so you can have some time with them, too," Piper offered optimistically.

"I can't. I need to figure out what my next move is, but I know it's not going back to Edenville. That place isn't home to me. I can't see myself going back."

"So you never planned to come back?" Josh asked, his face looking like he'd just taken a physical blow. Willow tried to hide behind the fact that she'd never promised him anything, but wasn't last night a silent agreement of some kind?

"Maybe I thought about it, but I know now I'm not."

"I wish I'd known that before last night, but I guess that's too much to ask from you, Willow. Some honesty," Josh murmured with an unfamiliar anger on his tongue.

"You said you came up here to find out what happened to these girls you remembered. Now you know." Bobby pointed that out as though it were the most obvious thing in the world. "You have nothing else to do here."

"Maybe I won't stay here, but it doesn't mean I have to go back to North Carolina, or Block Island, or school."

"Everything you said last night, hoping I could see through the murkiness in you that was bullshit?" Josh accused, and Willow felt her face go as gray as thundercloud. It wasn't that she hadn't meant what she said; it was that in the morning she wasn't as ready as she thought she'd be to live that truth.

"No. I didn't know last night what I planned to do. I didn't make any promises to you. All I can say is that I'm not going back there but I think all of you should. I'm fine now. I'll figure out what to do next." She knew she was not fine, far from it. But she also knew having them here wasn't going to change that one way or another. No one wants an audience when they're spiraling out of control.

"You ever notice that you make all your decisions without thinking of how anyone else might feel? That's a good way to end up alone," Josh shot back as he stood and stormed out of the restaurant.

"Aren't you going to go after him?" Bobby asked, looking at Willow like she had three heads.

"He's right. I do. Even if I went after him, what argument would I make? Listen, I do really appreciate the time you guys took and the fact that you gave up your honeymoon. It would have taken much longer to get to this point without you."

"Do you know the first time I met Piper, I had to chase her out of a diner just like this and apologize for being an ass? It's what makes what we have today possible," Bobby explained with a pleading tone.

"You don't understand," Willow argued as she dropped her fork loudly into her plate.

"You can tell everyone else they wouldn't understand, but that argument doesn't work on me," Piper cut in with an edge to her voice. "I'm one of the few people who understands what this moment feels like."

"I doubt it," Willow huffed back like a petulant child. By this point she was even annoyed with herself, but she didn't know how else to send all these people back to their lives and stop wasting their time. They had to hate her as much as she hated herself.

"You close your eyes and you see their faces. You remind yourself that all you would have had to do was speak up and they could be alive right now. When you start to feel happy, even if it's by accident, you remind yourself you don't deserve it. So you punish yourself. You push away what feels good because if those dead girls don't get to have it, neither should you." Piper laid out the scenarios in a way that made it clear she certainly did understand.

"I know this is what you're going to school for,

talking to people like me, but…"

"No you can't find this feeling in a text book," Piper interrupted, her face red with frustration. "For me it comes from watching my father kill my mother and then attempting to kill me. It comes from waking up in the hospital and being asked if I knew the person who attacked me because he was a serial killer they'd been hunting. It comes from being too scared and selfish to say anything." Piper's voice was growing louder and Willow watched as Bobby gently covered her hand with his, a simple act of comfort in a moment of pain. "Delanie Morrison will never have a chance to get married, but I will. She'll never have a chance to be loved by someone like Bobby because when my mouth was shut, my father was out killing her. I'll live with that every day of my life. I'll always see her face in the quiet moments of my life."

"I didn't know that," Willow said, swallowing hard.

"You know what else you don't know? That pain and my happiness are mutually exclusive of each other. I can carry both of them. You don't just walk through life. You can design your own if you're willing to work hard at it. I can go to Betty's every Wednesday for dinner and cuddle my godchild. Bobby can love me and I can love him back. You know what the difference between my story and yours is?"

"You're only talking about one girl," Willow said, staring down at the table, her cheeks blazing with a growing anger she couldn't pin down the source of.

"No. I was an adult. I was a full-grown person when I sat there and lied to the police about not knowing who attacked me. Ten years or more older than you were when you didn't speak up. But I've still managed to find a way to stop punishing myself. Finding my way in the world doesn't dishonor Delanie's memory, it does the opposite."

"And that's an epiphany you had, what, like the day after she was killed? Or a couple weeks later? You met Bobby and you just magically knew what to do?" Willow's voice was prickly with sarcasm. Though she was portraying these statements as accusations, they were actually questions. She wanted to know how Piper had managed to find her way but couldn't find the courage to just ask.

"No," Piper said, with a look of acknowledgement on her face. "You're right. It took some time. I made some wrong turns."

"I'm glad you've found a way to be happy Piper but excuse me if I'm still working on it," Willow blurted out as she got to her feet and headed for the door.

## *Chapter Fifteen*

"She is a pain in the ass," Bobby groaned, running his hand over his stubble-covered cheek. Josh, who had made his way back into the restaurant and flopped into the booth after Willow had left just nodded his head in agreement. "I don't know how you've been putting up with her," Bobby continued.

Josh shrugged as he pushed his eggs around his plate. "I guess it's time to ask myself why I am."

"She's in a rough patch," Piper sighed, though even she was starting to wonder if this was something Willow could pull herself out of.

"I don't think anyone would blame you Josh if you stopped chasing her. Maybe it's time to let her take care of herself," Bobby suggested.

"Where do you think I'd be if you'd given up on me when I kicked you out of my place and told you to go to hell?" Piper asked, raising an accusing eyebrow at Bobby.

"True." Bobby smiled as he wrapped his arm around Piper's shoulder. "But you were a little nicer than she's being."

"I think she's afraid to be nice, as if it will make us all like her and then she'll start to be happy. You'd be surprised how scary happy can be for some people," Piper explained. "Josh, we're heading home in the morning. Do you want to book the same flight as us?" Piper softened her face as she tried to imagine what it must feel like to be him right now.

"Thanks for the offer but my patients are covered and I'm not ready to go back. It might not be easy to understand why but I know exactly what's waiting for me back in Edenville. I've dated plenty of girls who aren't any trouble. The kindergarten teachers and the sweet librarians, they fit perfectly into my life the way it is today. The only problem is I don't fit there. Willow is different. She challenges me. It's harder to care about her, to understand her, but I feel like myself when I'm with her."

"That actually makes perfect sense Josh," Piper said, squeezing Bobby's leg below the table, partially to keep him from saying something insensitive but also to remind him that she hadn't been all that easy to love either.

"Then what's your plan?" Bobby asked, looking more skeptical than Piper.

"I guess I wait to see what her plan is. But I know it's not Edenville. I'll be there for the wedding though, I promise. No matter what she's got going on, I'll be there."

"Hopefully she comes too. But if she doesn't that isn't on you. The most important thing for you to remember is it's not your job to make her do anything. You can't force this to get better, you can just hope to be around when it does," Piper offered, channeling the memories of her own rough patches.

"I better go try to catch her at the hotel before she takes off to God knows where. Thank you both for everything you did. I can't imagine how long of a process this would have been if you hadn't stepped in." Josh tossed some cash on the table for breakfast and headed out the door.

"You think they're going to be all right?" Bobby asked as Piper leaned her weary head on his shoulder.

"Who knows? I still wonder some days if we're

going to be okay. I don't have the energy to speculate about anyone else's relationship."

"Since when do you worry about us? Getting cold feet?" Bobby asked, leaning away and looking down into her face.

"No, of course not. I can't wait to marry you." She leaned in and kissed his lips in a way that told him she was serious. "I guess I've been looking at Michael and Jules and wondering if that's ever going to be us?"

"Crazy? You want to be crazy like them?"

"They aren't crazy. They just work. You know what I mean? They have Frankie now and they look like they're exactly where they're meant to be."

"We'll be there some day. Little kids of our own running around. Our house will be all settled and we'll wake up one morning and know we're exactly where we're meant to be."

"After a week like this I really wonder if I want to bring a child into this world. Between both of us, we've seen so much. We know how bad it can be. I've been giving that a lot of thought. I'm not trying to spring this on you, I just think we should talk about it."

"I don't know if the craziness of the world is a reason not to have kids. There have always been problems; every generation has something. It's how you prepare and protect your kids that matters. I think we'll be great parents some day."

"I'm not saying I don't want to be parents, I'm just wondering if we should think through other options. Between my experience and everything I'm studying at school, I'm realizing how many kids in the world need help, need stability and love. I feel like maybe that's my calling. Our calling."

"I guess I never really gave it much thought. Adopting was a big part of my childhood. The time we had Jedda in our house was some of the best years of my life. Obviously it didn't turn out how we'd hoped but that wouldn't keep me from doing it myself. There are plenty of success stories out there. With our experience, I think adoption could be a great thing. I'd be open to it."

"Really?" Piper asked, looking unconvinced.

"Sure. I want you. I want a family. But nothing we've ever done has been entirely conventional. Why should we start now?" Bobby pushed his plate away and dropped some money on the table for the bill. "Let's pack up and get back to Edenville. I don't think there is much else we can do here."

"Do you think Betty would give us a hard time about adopting? She'll probably want us to have kids of our own."

"Are you kidding me? Betty will love the idea. She's been adopting all of us for years."

## *Chapter Sixteen*

"I wasn't sure I'd catch you," Josh said, standing in the doorway of the hotel room. Willow could feel the heat of his eyes on her and it was unnerving.

"I wasn't sure you'd try to," she answered, not able to meet his stare.

"Me either," he admitted as he leaned himself against the doorframe. It wasn't lost on her that he was blocking her exit. That was how she felt about him in general. He was the one thing that made her hesitate, made her think twice about cutting herself off from the world. But at the same time, it also made her feel trapped.

"So why did you?"

"Can we stop playing games Willow?" His voice was harsher than she'd heard it before and it made her feel guilty for putting him through this. "I love you, dammit. Even though you've given me almost no reason to. You've been in my brain since the first moment I met you and I can't get you out. Tell me right now, how do you feel about me? That's all I want to hear from you. Nothing else."

"I care about you, too," Willow conceded, looking more like she was being punished than proclaiming affection for someone.

"Don't look so happy about it." Josh muttered, and Willow's guilt grew.

"I'll put this in terms you might be able to understand. Imagine you had a disease; you were infected with something a long time ago and every day it eats away at you a little. Then the older you get the more you realize it's contagious. When you come into contact with

131

someone they don't make you feel better, you make them feel worse. You take bits and pieces of their happiness away from them. I care enough about you not to want to do that to you."

"Bullshit Willow. Don't give me that. Your analogy doesn't work. Because what you have isn't incurable. You just don't know today how to work through it. I'm willing to lose little bits of my happiness for now to help you. Because I believe you can get through this and when you do, I know we could have something."

"Maybe that's the part I like about you. The part that believes I can get well, be better. But it suffocates me right now to think about that."

"So what does that mean?"

"I don't know."

"The thing about loving you, Willow, is I can already see the running look in your eyes. I already know you're going, even if you don't want to admit it yet. Just don't lie to me."

Willow sucked in a breath and gave in to his penetrating stare. "I'm going back to California. It's the only place I've felt like my head was above water."

"That's because you were hiding. Hiding feels good for a little while but you can't live that way."

"I can try."

"I'm not going to chase you out there. I'm not going to follow you. If you walk away right now, I'm done. I can't want this more than you do. It's only fair that I let you know what's riding on your choice right now. I'll have your back wherever you want to go and whatever you want to do if we go together, but if you bail on me now, I'm done."

She knew he meant it as a threat, as an ultimatum but

really, it felt like a relief to know he was giving up. Not because she didn't desperately want him with her, but because she wanted better for him. She knew she'd likely regret it someday, maybe even sooner than she thought. But today, knowing the strings were all cut made her happy for him. She grabbed her bag and walked toward the door he was still blocking. This was the moment. The moment he'd step away, let her by, and not come after her. She could feel it.

"I'm sorry I couldn't be what you were hoping for," she sighed, keeping her face level, just inches from Josh's body.

"You're wrong, Willow. You're exactly what I was hoping for. You just didn't figure it out in time." He leaned down, pulled her in tight, and kissed her passionately, nothing at all like a last kiss. And she hoped that somewhere, somehow it wouldn't be.

## *Chapter Seventeen*

Being back in California, slipping back into her Claudia personality was like being wrapped in a warm blanket. Safe. Even though the time out here actually quite dangerous, it was emotionally sheltered. She'd still been paying rent on her crappy studio apartment, because a part of her knew she'd be back here.

She crashed on her bed, oddly comforted by the lumpy lopsided mess, and welcomed the quiet that followed. Staring over at the blank wall, full of pushpins and holes she couldn't believe everything that had been there was now gone. Solved. Resolved. But yet she felt worse. How could two people ruin so many lives? Her parents were truly patient zero in the disease she carried with her. It had poisoned so many. Jedda had lost so much. Those girls, and not limited to just the ones she remembered, had all been destroyed.

Rolling to her side, she looked down at her bag and saw a loose piece of paper that she didn't recognize. Josh must have slipped it in when he pulled her in for that goodbye kiss. She was afraid to look at it. She knew it was likely to reduce her to tears, but she couldn't help herself.

Unfolding it, she read the words slowly, knowing she might not hear anything else from Josh for a long time. This might be her last small connection to him. In his sloppy doctor's scrawl she read his message. Each day we are born again. What we do today is what matters most – Buddha.

She refolded the paper and placed it over her heart as she stared up at the ceiling. She'd never thought of life this way before. That today was the most important day of her life. That her choices now were as impactful as anything that had happened to her in the past. What she'd always thought was that the shape she'd taken on all these years was what made her who she was. As though she was stone and every day pieces were chipped away to form this damaged solid mass. But could it be that she was in fact clay? Malleable and able to start over each day, create her own shape, her own existence?

She contemplated the depth and perfection of those words as she slipped her shoes back on and headed for the door. If she were coming out here to be Claudia, then she'd need to see Marcario and maybe he'd have something worth hearing. Something that could snap her out of this. His wisdom was rooted in darkness but it often resonated with her. His palpable regret and pain spoke to her.

As she walked to the bar, she tried to imagine if this could be her life? How long could she stay in that apartment and sing at the bar? Maybe they'd pay her and that could be her job. She was out of pretty much all other money now and if that wasn't going to pay the bills she'd have to find something else.

Pulling open the heavy bar door she breathed in the scent of this place that she'd felt so comfortable in. This was where she was invisible and her history hadn't chased her down. It felt good to step into the bar and hear the familiar music chiming over the jukebox.

Marcario wasn't in his usual chair. As a matter of fact, none of his crew was where they normally were. The bar was not completely deserted but there weren't many faces familiar to Willow. She moved hesitantly, trying to read the situation.

"What are you doing back here?" Jose, the bartender asked as he quickly rounded the bar and grabbed her by the arm. He guided her to the room in the corner where Marcario occasionally held impromptu meetings usually resulting in shouting that could be heard in any corner of the bar anyway.

"I'm here to see Marcario," Willow said, yanking her arm back from his tight grip.

"This ain't his place anymore. His crew isn't welcome. And if these guys hear you used to roll with him you're screwed."

"What happened, why isn't his crew here anymore?"

"That's what happens when you get killed. Your turf gets taken over. Your crew gets bumped out."

"Who got killed?" Willow asked, boring holes through the man with her angry eyes. Not wanting to piece together what she was afraid he was telling her.

"Marcario got shot up. Right out front here. Streets say it was Big Bo who got wind of him ratting him out."

"No," Willow cried, bracing herself against a chair, nearly falling to her knees. "He can't be dead."

"He is, little girl and you need to get the hell out of here. He had a plan for his family and they're all taken care of but he told me if anything happened to him and you came back to take care of you too."

"Take care of me?" Willow asked, wondering if that was some sort of code for killing her.

"He left you some cash and said to make sure you go back home. Your real home. Block Island."

"What? I never told him where I grew up. He doesn't know me," she said, her breath labored.

The man walked over to a drawer in the corner of the room and pulled out a false bottom. There was an envelope in his hand and he shoved it into Willow's gut, as though she had better take it and run. "Go. Get out of here before anyone makes any connection."

Willow clutched the envelope and headed for the door, though she wasn't sure her legs would carry her. She broke into a full run. Sweat beading down her back as she headed for her apartment, making sure no one was following her.

Running up her steps, she pushed open her door and fell onto her bed, the tears already trailing their way down her face. She'd gotten Marcario killed. Her plan was the reason he was dead. It should be her. It was all her idea. The thoughts slammed into each other like train cars colliding.

After a few minutes of sobbing, the kind that hurts your stomach and stings your eyes, she fought to catch her breath and steady her emotions. The envelope she'd carried was still clutched in her arms. She was hugging it like she'd hug Marcario if he were here now.

She didn't love Marcario the way she did Josh. Her whole future wasn't buried in the depth of his eyes. But he'd helped her, protected her and let her escape into his world for a short time. Opening the envelope, she took in the musky smell of his cologne and it broke her heart. There were three stacks of bills, all held together with rubber bands and she dumped them out onto the bed, not knowing or caring how much was there. All she wanted was to read the words he'd left for her on the loose notebook paper folded up at the bottom.

Danielle Stewart

Willow,

Yes, I know who you really are. I've known since the first week I met you. I'm not stupid enough to do business with someone without knowing everything about them. I guess it doesn't matter though, if you're reading this then it really doesn't matter anymore. You're probably pissed, or mad at yourself or whatever but don't mourn me. This is what happens to guys like me. We have expiration dates out here.

I know you don't listen to anyone. But I bet you'll listen to a dead guy. Go back. I know what you went through. I know who you used to be. Who gives a shit? Go back and figure out who really has your back, and stop being so pissed. Stop chasing things that don't matter. If you came back here then you're running again and that really pisses me off. It means you didn't face something you were supposed to. Stop being a chicken shit. Stop running. Go back. Do whatever you didn't do. If I were here maybe I'd do it with you but I have a feeling whoever was on your mind last time I saw you, is probably still around. If he was man enough to keep you out of my bed then he must be someone worth sticking around for.

You're not Claudia, even if you want to be. It's not safe for you here. Go be Willow.

She folded up the paper and tossed it on the floor. It fell next the note from Josh, intended to remind her that every day can be a fresh start. A stark contrast to Marcario's note screaming that every day could be your

138

last. Neither on its own was a enough to cut to her core and make her actually think about changing direction, but together laying on the floor of her broken down empty studio apartment they were making an impact.

Marcario was dead. She wouldn't be running to the shelter of his world to hide. That bridge had fallen. Josh was back in Edenville, probably stepping back into his life and pushing the idea of Willow out of his mind. She looked down at the two notes and tuned into one line of Marcario's words, Go be Willow.

The only thing she didn't do in New Jersey was face her own history there. She'd found the answers to where the other girls who'd been chained to that wall ended up, but she didn't allow herself to remember what it was like when she was there. Willow had spent so long slicing that part of her life away, pretending it wasn't there anymore, that when she was given the chance she didn't take it.

She'd need to do it alone. Marcario was gone. She'd chased Josh off and while she had no doubt she could call him and he'd come help her she couldn't take him on that ride. He'd given her the chance and she walked away from him. Now it was up to her. She'd take a couple days in California, try to find some clarity on the beach as the waves rolled in, and then she'd head back to the city. She'd face the apartment. She'd go through her parents' belongings if there were any left. Maybe she'd known it all along, but facing that moment was what this was all about. It's what her life had been leading her towards. It was the tether that hitched her soul to the past and unless she got close enough to it, she'd never be able to sever it. It was time.

## *Chapter Eighteen*

The beach had actually helped, much to Willow's surprise. Soaking up the sun and bracing herself for what was to come was exactly what she needed. Now, as she stepped off the plane, she knew she couldn't get sidetracked. It would be easy for her to convince herself to go a million places besides the apartment, but if she didn't head there now she might never.

With any luck, Tony would be there and he'd let her in. And if not, then she'd park her butt outside and wait as long as it took. There would be no excuses, no stopping her. This place was a piece of her, a scar that couldn't be removed or covered but it didn't do her any good to pretend it wasn't there either. It ached and burned and it kept her from being able to give her whole heart to anyone. It made her snap, lash out, and push people away. It made her afraid. It made her conform and try too hard to be something she wasn't. It controlled her and she was tired of it.

The cab ride from the airport had her palms sweating and her nerves on edge. The closer she got to the apartment the heavier the weight on her chest grew. When the driver pulled up, she took cash from her bag and slapped it into his palm as she stepped out. None of this would even have been possible if not for the money from Marcario.

Staring up at the building as if it were the first time she'd seen it she took in a deep breath. Maybe the timing would be wrong. Maybe Tony went on vacation. She couldn't tell if she was hoping that was the case. Stepping forward she whispered to herself, you have to face this.

With fidgeting hands and sweat beading up on the back of her neck, she approached the door and rang the buzzer intended to call Tony down. When no one answered, she felt a wave of relief flood over her. She took a few steps backwards and spun quickly as she heard footsteps behind her.

"You're back?" Tony asked with a look of confusion on his face. "Your doctor friend said you might show up here."

"Josh?" Willow asked, stunned that the two would have talked again.

"Yeah, he left yesterday."

"What do you mean? He was here?"

"You bet he was. I don't know how he did it but he was down in that basement storage for two whole days sorting through everything. It took him almost a full day just to get to the back utility closet where I put all your old stuff."

"I don't understand."

"I told you, your parents' things were down there but they were so buried I didn't know how you'd ever get to them. Well he said that he thought you'd be back here one day to go through everything and he wanted to make sure you could get to them. I'll be honest, it's nasty down there. He came up out of that basement at the end of every day looking like he'd been working in a coal mine. That kid must really care about you to do that. But I didn't expect you back here so soon. He thought you'd maybe be back some time down the road, but not now."

"I've been scared," Willow admitted, her emotions making it impossible for her to block the truth from coming out. "I'm really scared."

A look of discomfort, swirled in with some empathy,

141

filled Tony's face. "Maybe you should call him. This doesn't sound like something you should do alone. I'm sure he'd come back."

"He would. But I can't ask him to. I wasn't very nice to him."

"It didn't seem to stop him from doing this for you," Tony reminded her, gesturing toward the house. "I know there is a lot of stuff down there. Maybe four or five boxes full. I'd hate to see you do that alone."

"Me too," Willow said, staring up at the cloudless sky. "Maybe I could get them shipped somewhere. My brother would want to see this stuff, too."

"I could help you with that. Josh moved them right out to the front of the basement. I could get my boy to help me carry them up. But I think it would cost a fortune to ship, they're heavy as hell."

"Maybe I'll rent a car and drive them down."

"Down where?"

"North Carolina."

"I think that would be a good idea."

"I still need to see the apartment though, I think." The shake in Willow's voice was telling.

"I'll let you in if you want, but can I tell you something?"

Willow nodded, unable to form any words for a second as her throat closed up with the thought of walking up the narrow brown stairwell toward her parents' house.

"This place isn't going anywhere. Nothing up there is changing. I don't mind letting you in, but I'll be honest, I'm not real good with emotions and stuff. You should have your people with you."

"My people?" Willow asked wiping the tears away.

"Yeah, you know the ones who were here the last time you tried. And maybe more. I don't care how many you bring, have a party up there for all I care. I think there are some things best done alone, but this ain't one of them. It's just my opinion. You do what you like."

Willow thought on it for a minute. Her people. Who exactly were her people? Josh? Bobby and Piper? Her adoptive parents whom she'd completely shut out? Betty? Jedda? When she really thought about it, if she had the guts to ask any of them they'd all drop what they were doing, lock arms with her and practically carry her up those steps if she needed it. Without deserving it, or knowing how it had happened, she had people.

"Maybe you're right," she relented as she stepped down off the porch and stood in the tall weed filled grass. She tilted her head up to see the window she'd spent so much time staring through. Turning toward the street she'd always looked out over, she was amazed how little the corner store had changed. Squinting, she focused in on a man leaning against the wall smoking a cigarette, pressed down tightly between two of his fingers. He pushed off the wall and walked a few steps as he greeted another man with a bump of their fists. The limp in his left leg brought her back to her childhood instantly.

"That guy, what's his name?" Willow asked, walking toward him without much thought.

"Where are you going?" Tony asked hurrying up behind her and catching her elbow. "Don't go over there. That's Lucian. He's trouble."

"I remember him. That limp, he's been hanging out there forever right?"

"He's a punk. Yeah, he's been hanging there for as long as I can remember. Why?"

143

"I just remembered something. He was with a girl for a while and then she was gone. I remember her," Willow said, thumping her palm to her forehead, trying to force the memories to come together.

"So?" Tony asked, shrugging his shoulders and not letting go of Willow's elbow.

"Someone recently showed me a picture of that girl but I'd forgotten her. I didn't make the connection. I'm sure of it now though," Willow asserted, nodding her head as the puzzle came together for her. "I need to go do something, but I'll be back for those boxes. If you can bring them up I'll be back in a day or two for them."

"Okay," Tony answered, looking completely confused. It didn't dissipate as Willow threw her arms around him for a hug. Something neither of them really expected would happen. "You're a nice man."

"Thanks," he stuttered, with a bashful smile that made Willow happy. Happy, she thought to herself acknowledging the wave as it swept her up.

She raced to the curb and had to fight the urge to cross the street and confront Lucian. She slipped her phone out of her pocket and snapped a picture of the man with the limp on the curb. She hailed a cab and headed for the only person she knew in the city that might be able to help.

## Chapter Nineteen

"I need to talk to him now," Willow demanded of the man in front of the police precinct. Finally, the he rolled his eyes and gestured for her to head back as he buzzed her in.

"Willow, what are you doing here?" Denny asked as he gathered up the gruesome crime scene photos he was analyzing and tucked them into a file.

"I need your help."

"Another bar fight?" he asked with a half-smile.

"No, I remembered something else and I need you to help me do it the right way. I thought about confronting the guy myself but I came here instead."

"That's a good choice. About time you started making some."

"Funny," Willow mused with a forced laugh. "Here, see this guy?" She flashed a photo from her cell phone toward Denny. "His name is Lucian. He hangs out in front of the place my parents lived. He has forever. When I was," she hesitated as she looked for the right words, "being kept at my parents' house I used to just look out the window for hours. I remember this guy with a girl. Then she was gone and so was he for a while and then he came back and she never did."

"Willow, that's not really a crime. I'm afraid I can't help you."

"Let me finish. A while back, that girl's sister, knowing that I had lived in that neighborhood, showed me a picture of the girl and asked for my help in finding her. The girl has been missing for years. She's never been found. Her family is still looking for closure. I didn't make the connection because I was only thinking of the girls in my parents' house. But when I saw him out there, it came back to me. I think he did something to her."

Denny took in deep breath and folded his arms across his chest. Willow braced herself for more objections and fully intended to fight her way past them. But she didn't need to. "What's the girl's name? Let's see what we can do."

"Thank you. Thank you so much."

"Don't thank me yet. Good chance you won't like this one either but I'm going to give it a try because, frankly, you've got a fire in your belly so few people have anymore."

"I really do want to do something. Anything that might help."

"Pull up a chair. Let's look her up and then we'll go have a chat with Lucian. I can't promise you anything but we can try."

"I feel good about this one, Denny," Willow announced with a wide smile. "I think we make a great team."

"Let's not get ahead of ourselves. I don't really do teams. But you can get the coffee or something."

## *Chapter Twenty*

It's funny how adrenaline can make a twelve-hour drive feel like a breeze. The weight of the boxes in the back seat of her rental car was slowing her down but nothing was going stop Willow from getting to that wedding. The last week had been life altering. It had made her feel things she never had before. Everything was stripped back and she had shed layers of herself she never knew she could. The last seven days she was Willow, in the truest form she'd ever experienced.

Every song on the radio was speaking to her. Every state she blew through got her closer to where she was desperate to be. When her eyes grew tired she reminded herself that she had no time to rest. Everyone would already have headed for the coast. They'd be there any minute and at the pace she was keeping, she'd be there just in time to see Piper walk down the aisle. She'd be wearing the jeans and T-shirt with a ketchup stain on it but she was hoping everyone would be able to overlook it.

Luckily, in true Betty fashion she'd gotten a voicemail two days earlier with all the wedding information just in case. And like usual that just in case had come to fruition. She knew where she was heading. She knew when she had to be there. The only thing she didn't have figured out was what the hell she was going to do or say once she was.

## Chapter Twenty-One

"You ready for this, brother?" Michael asked as he slapped Bobby on the shoulder, both of them dressed for the ceremony.

"I think I've been ready for this since the first time I saw her in the diner. I just hope she's ready."

"She is. I saw her this morning. So happy, so confident," Michael assured him as he cracked open a beer and passed it to Bobby then grabbed one for himself.

"Thanks for standing up with me today. I'm not sure we would have had much in common if it weren't for our two lunatic women, but I'm glad they're as crazy as they are so we can be friends."

"They are trouble makers but I wouldn't trade this for anything. We got pretty lucky. Hey speaking of crazy women, have you heard any updates on Willow? She still out in California?"

"I got a call from that detective in Jersey who helped us, saying he'd seen her and she was doing okay. So I guess she's back there. But I haven't told anyone else. It'll just drive Jedda nuts and I think Josh is barely over it. I don't want to drag him back to it."

"I saw him this morning; he looks like shit," Michael said as he adjusted his tie in the reflection of the glass door. They'd been banished to the back porch of the beach house so the women could get ready. Jedda and Clay were good enough to get everything set up for the ceremony out by the water. Chairs. The arbor, the trail of flowers over the sand that would serve as an aisle.

Bobby and Piper had decided on simple, as absolutely simple as Betty would allow. They'd have been perfectly happy packing a lunch, everyone piling in the car and heading to the courthouse for a quick and informal eloping ceremony. But of course, that wouldn't fly with Betty. A certain level of pomp and circumstance was still required, even if it was just for her sake. She'd earned it after all. They'd all put her through the emotional ringer over the years. Loving them, worrying about them, it was no small task and she did it tirelessly. The least they could do was stand up in front of her and all the people they love and commit themselves to each other.

"Boys," Betty's voice sang as she peeked her head out the screen door and looked them over. "Bobby, for goodness sake, your tie looks like it was tied by a blind ape. Get over here." She stepped out and immediately yanked him over by the collar to get him squared away.

He looked into her face as she worked with a look of determination to fix the mess he'd made of it. "You ever stop cleaning up after everyone?" Bobby asked as she tightened the knot and laid it flat with a gentle push of her hand.

"I sure hope not. That'll be a sad day when no one needs me anymore," her eyes glazed over for a moment as she brushed some invisible lint off the sleeve of Bobby's coat.

"Good thing you associate yourself with a group who can't seem to keep themselves out of trouble. One of us gets sorted out and two more show up with something for you to worry about." Michael grinned as he stepped toward Betty, allowing her to straighten his already perfectly straight tie.

"Speaking of which, anyone heard from Willow? I sent her the information for the wedding but I didn't hear

149

back." Betty said, in a hushed voice.

"It's okay," Bobby shrugged. "Thank you for trying, but we have lots of people here. I'm so glad Marty and his family could come. It's nice having my parents here and seeing them with Jedda again. It's like going back in time to when he first moved in with us. I can almost imagine what it would have been like if none of the bad stuff happened and we all just ended up right here. Time helps. It's why I believe Willow will eventually come around."

"She will," an out of breath voice called from behind them. They all turned to see Willow looking harried and bending to relieve the cramp in her side from running down the long driveway toward the house.

"Willow, you made it," Bobby cried out, pulling her in for a hug. "Are you okay?"

"I'm fine. Just out of breath," she huffed into his shoulder as his arms closed tighter around her. He'd already resigned himself to her not coming, and the sight of her here now was stirring his already raw emotions.

"I'm so sorry I'm late, and I look like crap. I don't have anything to wear. I can stand in the back or something," she apologized as she looked down at her messy clothes. "I actually just needed to tell you something and I didn't want it to wait. I need your advice."

"No way," he said, shaking his head assertively. "Not about the advice, that's fine. But you aren't standing somewhere in the back. Betty you can do something right? I want her standing up with me."

"With you?" Willow asked furrowing her brows.

"Yes. Michael is my best man, and Jedda is standing with me. I want you up there too."

"Why?"

"We have a bond, Willow. Jedda is our brother and as far as I'm concerned, you showing up here today makes you my sister. It means the world to me and I want you up there. You're my family."

"I," Willow bit at her lip and finally just nodded her head in agreement when the words couldn't be found.

"Let's go find you something to wear." Betty rejoiced, locking her arm in Willow's and tugging her toward the house.

"Someone should warn her," Michael said and it had Willow digging her heels in and turning around to try to decipher his comment.

"Warn me about what?"

"Your parents are here," Michael said calmly and directly. "I thought you should know."

"They are?" she asked in a tiny, childlike voice and turned to Betty as though she'd have something supportive to say. And like usual she did.

"Child, if the worst thing you have to face in a day is your wonderful parents, then you'll be fine. I've had the pleasure of spending a morning with them and they are truly lovely people. They have the one thing you need in parents."

"What's that?" Willow asked, leaning in slightly toward Betty for support

"Absolute unconditional, no strings attached kind of love. It's not easy to do and it's even harder to find, but they've got it. So I know you'll work it out."

"I hope you're right," she sighed, as she stepped into the house.

"With my track record, the odds are in your favor sweetie. I'm always right."

"I wonder what she needed your advice on?" Michael asked taking a long swig of his beer.

"Well with her track record it doesn't matter, she wouldn't take my advice."

"She seems different," Michael offered, leaning against the rail of the porch.

"She does," Bobby agreed as he clanked the side of his beer against Michaels. "Maybe another broken person all fixed up? I'm starting to think we might be onto something here. Maybe we can save the world."

"Let's just try to keep our little world safe and calm for a while before we try to conquer anything else."

"I can live with that."

## *Chapter Twenty-Two*

Willow tried on seven dresses before settling on the simple cream-colored eyelet capped sleeved one.

"Tell me again why you have this many dresses here in my size?" Willow asked Betty as she stepped out of the bathroom. She laughed as Betty let out a happy gasp at the site of her in the dress.

"I'm a firm believer in being prepared for all types of scenarios. But I'll be honest I was pleasantly surprised to need one of these dresses. I've known a lot of people in my life but you're the first to flat out call me a bullshitter."

Willow felt the heat rise in her cheeks as she thought back to what she'd said on the phone to Betty while she was drunk. "I am truly sorry about that Betty. I was so angry."

"I know child, no need to apologize. I like that spark you have in you. I think if you can harness that and use it for good you could move mountains."

"Can I ask your advice on something? Well two things really."

"Of course." Betty said, patting the bed next to her and Willow settled shoulder to shoulder with her.

"I have something really important to tell everyone but I'm afraid my timing is wrong. I don't want to keep it for another minute but I also know this is Bobby and Pipers day."

"Well just ask yourself what Bobby and Piper would want. It is their day, but they aren't the type of people who mind sharing it with others. Neither needs much of a spotlight on them. As a matter of fact I'm quite certain this wedding is more for me than for them."

"Okay, I'll think about it," Willow said, nodding her head. "But the second thing isn't so easily fixed."

"Josh," Betty said knowingly with her lips pursed.

"Yes. I don't deserve him and I think I blew it with him. My head keeps telling me the humane thing to do for his heart is let him go. I had my chance. I made my choices."

"But?" Betty asked with a raised eyebrow.

"My heart keeps telling me to fix it, if I don't I'll regret it the rest of my life. I've never met anyone like him before. He's so genuine. He gives everything he has without a second's hesitation. And every time he has, I've stomped on that. Why would he trust me again to not do the same thing again? How will he ever believe I won't just run?"

"My mama used to tell me that wherever I go in this world to listen to the sense the good Lord gave me, but to never leave home without my heart. Life without love is like the sky without the sun. It's important to listen to your brain, but it's crucial to follow your heart."

"He told me he loved me. I didn't say it back."

"Are you sure you didn't?" Betty drawled with a grin.

"Um, I mean I know when I called you I was pretty drunk, but I didn't spend the whole time out there on a bender. I think I'd remember if I said I loved him."

"I know you didn't say the words, but that's not the only way to say it. There are acts of love that speak volumes."

"I didn't do any of those either. I was a bitch."

"Pushing someone away because you know you aren't ready to love them. That's an act of love. Trying to

154

right your past so that you can be worthy of their emotions for you, that's an act of love. The words are important Willow but they aren't everything."

"I never thought of it like that," she whispered feeling a layer of guilt peel away from her. "But maybe he hasn't thought of that either. Maybe he's still furious."

"I've known many men in my life," Betty said patting Willow's leg. "Well not like that, that's not what I meant." She blushed slightly, making Willow laugh out. "I just mean I've come in contact with, oh you know what I mean. Josh is special. He's different. Not many men would do what he's done for you. Or if they did, they'd have expected something in return or played the martyr when it didn't work out the way they wanted. When Josh came back here, it wasn't about what you'd done to him it was about what you were doing to yourself. There are few people in the world who can value you more than they value their own happiness. That's the proof of an amazing person, when they can see the beauty in those around them, even when it's buried. When you find that, you wrap your arms around it and hold on for as long as life lets you. He wants you happy. If you can do that, you'll give him everything he needs."

"For the first time in a long time, I feel like I can do that. Something happened in the city Betty. A miracle. It started to change me."

"Then don't let anything stop that change. Think of it like a wave. You've been at sea a long time Willow. Ride that wave to shore, because we're all here waiting for you."

"I will," she whispered, letting the tears roll down her cheek. "I am going to be better."

"Just remember Willow you don't have to be perfect,

you just have to be present. No one cares what trouble you're feeling while you're here, they just want to be with you. You've been through more than anyone should have to go through in ten life times. You should have been worried about the monsters under your bed, not the real life monsters walking this earth. You didn't get a fair shake, but you've got something now you didn't have before."

"What's that?" she asked, leaning her head on Betty's shoulder and taking the tissue she was offering. The woman really had everything covered all the time.

"An army. You have the love and support of an army now. There will never come a day when you will be alone, even if you want to be. Bobby just called you his sister. I've seen what he does for people he considers family. I've benefited from it myself and so has Jules. There is no turning back now. Our love is like a disease and you've been infected. There's no cure. You've got us for life," she wrapped her arms around her and squeezed with the tightness of a boa constrictor.

Willow thought back to the analogy she used to try to push Josh away, oddly similar though the polar opposite. She'd thought herself such a plague that she couldn't be around anyone without bringing them down. But in fact, this love was more powerful than anything she'd thought was inside of her. She really believed no matter what she did now, nothing could cure Willow of Betty's love. And as she embraced Betty tightly, sobbing like a fool into her shoulder she realized this was something she never wanted to be cured of.

When she finally composed herself she stood and brushed the tears from her cheeks.

"Good thing I didn't do my makeup yet," she said,

an attempt at levity in a powerful moment. "Do you think they know I'm here yet?"

"We banished Bobby and Michael to the back porch so I doubt they told anyone yet. Josh is helping set up the chairs and stuff with Jedda and Clay. I'm sure they're finished by now. I can send him up."

"No, I'm not ready. I need to see my parents first. I owe them a million apologies." Willow slapped her hand to her forehead. "And like twenty thousand dollars."

"Then I'll send them up. Don't be afraid Willow. Don't be afraid of their love for you."

Those words pierced the armor of Willow's heart with a sting she wasn't prepared for. That was something no one had ever said to her before. She'd given herself a thousand reasons why she fled Block Island. It was her inability to be healed the way they wanted her to. It was the embarrassment she'd brought on them. But in reality, their love terrified her. It was so pure and without any type of reservation that at times, it felt like it could not possibly be real. Much like Josh's love. She could not only accept that kind of love, but maybe she could learn to give it as well. Surely, with so many teachers, it was a skill she could learn.

A quiet knock on the door sent Willow almost instantly to tears. She knew it was her mothers' delicate kind hand on the other side and she was suddenly desperate to be in her arms. She croaked out the words "come in," and drew in a deep centering breath.

The sight of her mother and father stepping quietly in, their hands locked together sent a scared shiver through her body. She'd thought through what they might say, what she might say but it all evaporated at the sight of them. "I'm so sorry," she cried as she raced to them and felt their arms close in around her. All three were in tears as she breathed in the scent of them.

"It's okay, monkey," her dad said into her ear, the name she earned for hiding in trees on days she was scared just after her adoption. Hearing him utter those words, knowing he still held that affection for her was all she needed in that moment. The last strength she had in her legs began to fade away and all her weight was on them now. They moved toward the bed and all sat, as close as physically possible.

"I just had some things I needed to do and I didn't know how to tell you what was going on with me. I thought you would be mortified that it had gotten out on the news about me, about where I was really from. We kept it secret for so long." Willow's words flowed together and she hoped they were making sense.

"Oh, baby stop," her mother said, pulling her in, her hand wiping away her own tears and then Willow's. "We never kept your past a secret for our sake. We took our lead from you. We didn't think you wanted people to know so we supported you. But neither of us has ever been embarrassed or ashamed of who you are. You make us proud every single day. Even on your worst day. You're our miracle."

"What?" Willow asked pulling away and looking back and forth between the two of them.

"All we ever wanted was a child. You saved us. You gave us new life, a family," her father choked out. "You're all we ever wanted."

"But I stole from you. I ran away. People on the island must be driving you crazy with all the gossip."

"Who gives a shit?" her mother replied, uttering the first swear Willow had ever heard her say. "That money was your college money. It was yours, and if you did something with it that you felt you needed to, then that's fine by us. We wished you hadn't run off but believe it or not your father and I both had our struggles over the years and we've done our share of running, sometimes it's just what you need to do."

"As for the gossip," her father cut in, "the only phone calls we've gotten are from our friends asking what they can do to help, telling us they support and love us."

"Really?" Willow asked in disbelief. "People aren't wondering why you let someone like me into your house? They aren't asking about Jedda?"

"They are asking about Jedda, they're asking if he's all right and if he needs anything now that he's out. They're calling him a hero for saving you. So are we. We've had the pleasure of spending the morning with him and your mother cried all over him, just thanking him for what he did for you."

"You look so much alike," her mother choked out. "It made me miss you even more. I didn't think you were coming today. But I wanted to be here just in case. I wanted to be here because I wanted to be with other people who love you as much as I do. If I couldn't see you then that was the kind of company I wanted to keep."

"I love you both so much. I don't know what I would have done without you. You saved me and I just wish I'd acted worthy of it. But I promise you, I'm going to be."

"You just have to stop trying Willow. Stop trying to be what you think we want you to be and just be who you are. We love you already. You don't have to earn that. You just have to let us."

"I will," she said, pulling them both in tighter to her.

Another knock at the door sent them all wiping at their cheeks and trying to gather themselves.

Jedda poked his head in and then at the sight of Willow, charged forward, not waiting to be invited in. "I knew you were here. I saw Betty talking to your parents and I knew you were here," he said as she sprang up and fell into his arms.

"I'm sorry Jedda. I know I wasn't very good to you when you needed me. You've always done everything to protect me and I threw that in your face."

"I love you Willow," he said, his safe large arms encompassing her in a way that made her feel like a little girl again. "I'd do anything for you."

"I didn't know how to deal with that."

"I know. And Bobby told me it didn't really work out up there in the city. There weren't any happy endings. That must have been hard. I wish I could have been with you."

"What do you mean?" her father asked, and Willow realized they didn't know what the last few months had been like for her. She'd completely shut them out and they deserved more than that.

"I went back to where I was born and tried to piece together what I remembered about what my parents did. There were some girls, they sold them, and I was trying to figure out where they might be. If I could do anything to help them."

"You did that by yourself?" her mom asked in a concerned voice as she covered her heart with her hand.

"No, I wasn't alone. I haven't been alone since I met all these crazy people," Willow said gesturing out the window to where the wedding would be. "But unfortunately the girls either didn't survive or didn't have happy endings. My parents destroyed their lives."

"Oh my gosh, Willow, that must have been devastating," her father said reaching out and grabbing her shaking hand.

"It was but it didn't end there. I did find two happy endings."

"You did?" Jedda asked, clearly not knowing what might have changed from Bobby's last update.

"I'll tell you all about it later. I actually brought all the stuff from our old apartment back with me. I was hoping you would go through it with me. But we've got to get cleaned up and ready for this wedding. Bobby's asked me to stand up with him. I can't do that with these circles under my eyes."

"Of course I will. And I'll be up there with you today," Jedda said, stealing one last hug before he and Willow's father headed out of the room.

"Will you help me get ready mom," Willow asked and loved the light that filled her mother's face.

"I can't think of anything better in the world," she said brushing Willow's hair away from her eyes and studying her face as if she couldn't believe this was more than a dream.

"Can I tell you something, Mom?"

"I hope you tell me everything Willow. I hope you talk and never stop."

"I think I'm in love."

"Oh please, tell me it's Josh. I only picked up bits and pieces of what happened but he's so handsome. Is it him?"

"It's him," Willow smiled as her mother stood behind her. She looked at their reflections in the mirror. "I'm afraid I don't really know how to be in love, and I might have ruined things already but I'm going to try."

"With the right guy, that's all you need to do is try, and the rest works itself out. Do you have anything planned for how to tell him?"

"I have no idea, but I'm hoping it comes to me."

Her mom wrapped her arms around Willow's waist and rested her chin on her shoulder, their cheeks pressed together. "I'm never going to give up on you."

"Promise?" Willow asked as she smiled at their reflection.

"Promise."

## Chapter Twenty-Three

The waves were crashing rhythmically against the shore as Willow gazed upon the most beautiful wedding she'd ever seen. The crowd was small but so brimming with love. There were no neighbors of a great aunt, but only those who truly were meant to be there. Willow had stayed upstairs getting ready until the ceremony was just about to start. She didn't want to admit it was to avoid Josh but it was. The timing to talk to him wasn't right and she didn't want to waste her chance.

When she walked down the aisle with her arm in Jedda's she looked up at the arbor, the backdrop of the ocean and saw the look of surprise on many faces. Jules had clearly been given the heads-up by Michael, but Crystal looked completely shocked and then instantly thrilled to see she and Jedda arm in arm. Behind her and Jedda, she heard Piper's voice, saying her name. She turned to see her arm locked with a man that she'd never met but that so closely resembled Piper that she knew they must be related.

"Wait!" Piper shouted as she shook her arm free and charged halfway up the aisle toward Willow. Jedda let her go and Piper's arms were around her in an instant. "Thank you so much for coming." Piper sang as she squeezed her tighter.

"Piper," Willow said quietly, "go back over there and walk down the aisle the right way. It's kind of important."

"She doesn't do anything the right way the first time," Bobby said with a smile, the gleam of tears in his overjoyed eyes.

163

As if she suddenly realized where she was, Piper's face grew pink and she hustled back to her father's arm. "Sorry about that," she said as she passed the small crowd of people who'd come to share their special day.

When Willow got to the front of the aisle, she hugged Bobby tightly and stood to his right, just on the other side of Michael, who threw a wink her way. "Good choice kid," he whispered and for some reason his approval sent a wave of joy over her. Her choices had put him at a legal risk too and through the reckless moments of her past few months, she felt immensely guilty about that.

Her eyes locked with Josh's, whose face was giving no indication of his emotions. She wished he wasn't so in control of himself. She wished she could read his heart by the look on his face so she knew what she was up against, but there were no clues painted there.

As the bridal march began, everyone got to their feet and her eyes moved from Josh to Piper. During her time in the city with Piper and Bobby, Willow found out more about Piper's plight and knowing that a path so jagged could still lead to a place so happy gave her hope for herself.

She listened intently to every word, every vow, and every moment of the wedding. She took it in like a warm drink on a cold day.

When Bobby and Piper were proudly pronounced husband and wife, the small crowd cheered in a way that spoke volumes about the journey these two had been on. Bobby kissed Piper with such enthusiasm that he lifted her off her feet. At that, the group cheered even louder. So loud in fact, that it stirred little baby Frankie, who was quickly soothed by a doting Betty.

As Bobby and Piper charged back down the aisle amid flying rice and cheers Willow covered her heart with her two hands and relished the happiness that was today. She thought hard about what Betty had said about sharing her big news on a day that belonged to Piper and Bobby and she'd realized that most people wouldn't appreciate it, but most people were not Piper and Bobby. She imagined they would feel blessed to know their big day was shared with someone else's big news.

"Okay everyone let's move to the tables for some tasty beach food!" Betty clapped as she handed Frankie over to Jules and slipped her hand into Clay's. Everyone began heading down toward the water where the tables stood covered in newspaper in preparation for the southern boil about to be enjoyed.

Willow searched the small crowd for Josh and spotted him heading down to the tables with the other guests. He was not waiting for her, not glancing back to see where she was. For the first time she was searching for him and now, he wasn't searching for her.

"Josh," she called loudly and she didn't care that every head turned her way, as long as his did too. And it did. His flat expression was still mystifying her. It gave no indication of what she should expect, though she was starting to assume it wasn't good.

He stopped and the crowd passed by him but he didn't make a move to come back toward her so she went to him. She wanted to wrap her arms around him but she held back, his body language suggesting such a gesture wouldn't be welcomed.

"I have a lot to say to you, but I can't tell if you want to hear it," she said quietly as the last few wedding guests fell out of earshot.

"I'm glad you came today. It's good for your parents, it's good for your brother. But I don't think it's great for us. So I think I might just head out. This is your family, you should be here, but I don't need to be."

"No," she said with an urgency that changed the look on his face for just a split second. "Please don't leave. I have news, big news. Good news. And I need you to hear it."

"I think you've confused my compassion for weakness Willow. Maybe that was my mistake. Know that I'm kind to everyone, but I'm not weak. I'm not a doormat."

"I know that. I'm weak. I've been stupid and weak but something happened in the city and it changed me. I feel like it changed everything. I want another chance. Just don't leave yet. Please. I have so much to say to you."

"Fine," Josh shrugged, "but now isn't really the time for us to sit here and argue it out. Whatever you have to say, I don't want to hear it now." He turned on his heels and she watched as his footprints in the sand left a trail behind him. She fought the urge to cry, remembering that she'd hurt him and it was perfectly fair for him to be upset.

Her mom stepped to her side, coming from who knows where to rub her hand in a comforting circle on her back. "It's okay Willow. He'll come around."

Willow nodded and smiled as they headed toward the water to join everyone. She hadn't been hopeful that her first attempt at an apology would work. She was prepared to say a hundred I'm sorrys if that's what it took. Josh was worth it.

## *Chapter Twenty-Four*

Piper could feel the champagne going straight to her head and she hoped that it wouldn't dull the memory of this utterly perfect day. A day she never believed she'd have a chance to experience in her lifetime. She'd had her first dance with her husband. She'd had her dance with her father. She'd grown her family exponentially just by allowing herself to be loved. Something so many people rob themselves of. Something so many people convince themselves they don't deserve.

As Jules stood to give her toast, she handed Frankie to Betty and raised her glass.

"Piper, you are a weirdo," Jules started, and everyone laughed. "You take the path less traveled. You don't stop until the job is done. You challenge us all to do the same. I've known Bobby a very long time and though he's always been a good guy, you've helped him be a great man. I know as I sit here today that I'm witnessing the start of a great love. Michael and I are so blessed to have you in our lives. Frankie is so blessed to have you both as godparents. You are truly my sister, Piper. I hope our lives are calm from this point forward. We've all earned that. But if they aren't I can't think of any other people I'd like to be with when things get crazy." She raised her glass and everyone did the same as they toasted the bride and groom.

Michael stood next and raised his glass ready to toast Bobby. "In the eloquent words of my dear wife, Bobby you are also a weirdo," And the group erupted in laughter again. "Which makes you perfect for each other. I think being in love when times are good is easy. But fighting

167

for love, teaching each other how to be the best version of yourself, that's the truest form of love. You and Piper have that in spades. A little over a year ago I was just kind of floating through life. Working, hanging out, really with no purpose at all. And it seems like I closed my eyes and woke up here. Surrounded by friends and family. Like it fell from the sky and I'm the luckiest guy in the world. You're a big part of that. You're my best friend. We've had to put up with these girls and their crazy adventures, and I know I couldn't have done that without you." Michael raised his glass a little higher. "To Piper and Bobby."

Piper hadn't been much for tears over the years but this was a day she'd decided it was pointless to fight it. She'd sprung for the expensive waterproof mascara and allowed herself to just feel all the feelings that came to her. As Michael made his way back to the table, Piper pulled him in for a hug and whispered in his ear. "Who knows where I'd be if you hadn't carried me out of that bar that night. I was so in over my head that I went and let someone slip something in my drink. Thank God you were there."

"Saving your ass is one of my favorite hobbies," he bragged, kissing her cheek affectionately.

"Thank goodness."

The older generation of guests moved into the house for coffee and to sit and chat, while everyone else gathered around the fire. Piper on Bobby's lap, she now changed out of her wedding dress, his tie long since removed. The baby had gone inside with Betty leaving Michael and Jules to relax, both sipping on a drink and looking like they'd been waiting for it all day. Jedda and Crystal were standing, laughing at some quiet joke that made everyone turn and take note of how much more frequently Jedda's laugh could be heard lately.

"Do you mind if I say something," Willow asked, looking uncomfortable as every eye turned toward her.

"Of course not," Bobby said, shoving her forward slightly.

"I don't know if this is even the right moment or not. I'm terrible at these things. This is your day and I don't want to take away from it at all. But I asked Betty and her advice was to think about what you two would want. And from what I know about you two, you understand that happy endings are hard to find and you have to fight for them. So I have some good news, and rather than pulling the person aside and telling them one on one, I want to tell them right here while we're all together. Is that okay?" she asked looking at Bobby and Piper like she might throw up.

Piper grinned widely, still so happy to see Willow here that she almost didn't care what the girl did. "I have no clue what you're getting at Willow but if you have any kind of good news, we want to hear. Today really isn't just about Bobby and me because it's taken the support of so many people to get us here. We'd be nowhere without that. Please, whatever it is, we want to hear it."

"Okay," Willow started, her hands shaking like leaves in the wind. "I was an ass to you and I'm really sorry," Piper waived her off and Willow got herself back on track. "But that's not what I want to tell you. This is actually for Crystal."

"What?" Crystal asked, nearly spilling her drink at the sound of her name. She and Jedda were standing by the recently lit fire dug into the sand and now both had a look of fear on their faces.

169

"I went back to the apartment that Jedda and I were born in I couldn't go in. I tried a few times but I never made it past the door. The last time I was there, I was standing outside and I saw someone familiar. A guy who hung out there for like ever and seeing him brought back a memory for me. I remember a girl with him, the girl in the picture you showed me Crystal. Your sister."

## Chapter Twenty-Five

Willow paused on the words and braced herself against the wave of emotion that came over Crystal's face. It was like nothing she'd ever seen before. It could only be described as disbelief veiled over a small flicker of hope.

"Are you sure?" Bobby asked, switching from groom to cop in a matter of seconds.

"I'm positive. The man's name is Lucian," Willow explained with a smile that did nothing to calm Crystal's conflicted face. Clearly too afraid to be happy, and too shocked to be still, she jumped closer to Willow and Jedda was a step behind her.

"I remember him," Jedda said, closing his eyes, looking like he was conjuring up the memory. "A scrawny guy with a limp right?"

"If you can identify him we'll go in the morning Crystal," Bobby assured her as she stumbled forward, bracing herself on Jedda's arm. "I'll call Denny, we'll get the guy in for an interrogation. He may know something pertinent."

"He does," Willow informed them with a dancing joy in her eyes. "Denny's already brought him in for questioning."

"And?" Crystal cried her eyes overflowing with tears as she drove her fingernails into Jedda's arm.

"He told us what happened. Your sister had started hanging out there over the summer. I guess she wasn't getting along with your parents."

"They were strict, but they're good people." Crystal said, and Willow instantly felt guilty if Crystal felt her

171

words were an acquisition.

"They are, I'm sure. I didn't mean to say it was their fault. I just wanted you to know what Lucian had to say. Your sister started dating a guy, Cy Relter. She got pregnant. Cy wanted her to get rid of the baby and she was too afraid to tell your parents. But she didn't know what to do. She took the money that Cy gave her and instead of getting it taken care of, she went to Lucian for help. He got her a new identity. He helped her get out of the city. He's no hero, but he's greedy and that's why he helped her. He gave us the name of her new identity and Denny was able to track her down. She's alive." Willow said in a voice that didn't sound like her own. It was light and full of elation. Happy news was so much easier to deliver than anything else.

"She is?" Crystal asked, folding in over herself and sobbing into Jedda's arms. "She's alive?"

"I spoke to her myself," Willow said, moving toward Crystal and taking her hand, wanting to ground them both in this moment. "She can't wait to see you."

"Where has she been, why hasn't she come home? My parents, they've refused to sell their house because they didn't want to be gone if she ever came home?" Crystal begged, a frantic confusion on her face.

"We talked a lot about that, and I could really relate to her. You start off one way, feeling scared and embarrassed and then it just seems like too much time has passed to ever make it right again. You convince yourself everyone is better off without you. It just gets away from you."

"Where is she? Is she okay?" Crystal asked, her mind clearly buzzing with the unknown.

"She's in Ohio and she sounded like she was doing

really well. She has a family, two older kids in their teens and a toddler. She's married."

"Kids? This doesn't make any sense. She should have called or come home." A look of anger spread across Crystal's face and Willow had prepared herself for this. Who wouldn't be hurt if they spent so much of their life looking for their missing sister? Grieving. Mourning. Working tirelessly to find her. After all, it's what really brought Crystal to Edenville, though in the end her love for Jedda is what kept her.

"But she's alive," Josh interjected, stepping to Willow's side, but not close enough for her to feel him against her. "Willow and I spent time in the city, listening to how these things normally turn out. The statistics would crush you. She's alive Crystal and that's all that matters."

Those were the words Willow would have used if Josh hadn't stepped in to say them. But she was glad he had, it meant when she looked like she might falter he still wanted to be next to her. "She's waiting for your call." Willow handed over her cell phone as she queued up the number.

Crystal snatched the phone away as if it were a treasure that might disappear if she blinked. She looked at Jedda as though she needed to be assured she wasn't dreaming. "Right now? I don't want to leave the wedding."

"You better," Piper called pointing her finger toward the ocean. "Right now. Go, call her."

Jedda smiled down into Crystal's face as he put his arm around her. He led her shaking legs down toward the serine water and everyone grinned widely as they watched them go.

173

"A happy ending," Josh murmured in a hushed voice only for Willow to hear. The lightness in his tone was a small blessing. It made her hope he'd listen to her apology. Even if he didn't want to accept it, at least he'd hear it.

"Can you believe it?" she asked, turning slightly toward him but not brave enough to face him full on.

"You went back to the apartment again?" he asked, seeming reluctant but unable to keep himself from asking.

"Yes. I went out to California thinking maybe that would be a good place to lose myself. Marcario," Willow swallowed hard realizing this would be the first time she'd have to utter the words. "He was killed. He left me a note telling me that he knew exactly who I was, and to stop trying to be any different. His words, and yours, they were enough to bring me back there. I planned to go into the apartment and just face it. Then Tony told me what you did. How hard you worked. You did that even though you thought there was no future for us. You did it when it had no benefit for you. Without knowing if I'd ever be back there. That's when I knew I was crazy to push you away."

"I'm sorry to hear about your friend. It must have been hard finding that out." Josh consoled as he reached his hand up, but dropped it before they could touch. "So you already looked through the stuff from your parents' house? Did you go in the apartment?" he asked changing the subject.

"No," Willow hung her head as a knot of regret tightened inside of her. When she was standing in front of the apartment, it felt like an insurmountable task, but when she left it, she always kicked herself for not going

174

in. "I have the boxes in my trunk. I'm going to have Jedda go through everything with me. I think it will be better if we do it together. I didn't go in the apartment either. I couldn't."

"It's better that you didn't go alone. You made the right choice."

"So I'm one for a hundred on that. Maybe a thousand. I was hoping some time, if you do decide to forgive me, you'll come back with me. That we could try to go in there together."

"Whether you and I have a future together or not, I'd still go with you if that's what you wanted."

"Thanks," Willow said as a small pain pierced her heart. She didn't want to think of a scenario where they didn't have a future. She didn't want to believe that could be an option. "I talked to my parents too. They were surprisingly great about everything. I think I might be getting back on track."

"I'm glad," Josh said with a snap in his voice, but his face showed regret for it almost immediately. "I really am glad Willow. It's what I wanted for you."

"And for us?"

"The magical thing would be for us to walk down by the water and pretend we hadn't said all the things we had. Tonight would be the storybook way to fix it all. But unfortunately, I'm too logical for all that. I wasn't blessed with that streak of imagination. None of this is going to be resolved here tonight. I don't trust you not to run again."

"That's fair," Willow resigned as she nervously wrung her hands. "You waited for me. I'll wait for you, and if you never trust me again, I'll understand."

"Willow," Michael walked up and broke the moment

Danielle Stewart

between her and Josh. He quickly read the situation and looked apologetic as he continued. "Oh, sorry. I just wanted to tell you I'm really proud of you. But I'll come back." His cheeks were rosy from the indulgence of a few too many drinks and he stumbled back slightly, Josh catching his arm.

"No, you stay Michael I'm going to go grab another drink. Can I get you one?"

"No more for me." He grinned and spun back toward Willow. "Sorry, I didn't mean to interrupt there. Bad timing."

"There really wasn't anything else to say, so maybe your timing was perfect. I really blew it with him."

"You are a pain in the ass," Michael joked as he nudged her with his elbow. "But your one of us now, so you're in the company of professional pains in the ass. It'll work out."

"I'm not sure I deserve him."

"I know everything about all of these people," Michael whispered, pointing out to the group of laughing friends who were enjoying the warmth of the fire and the sand between their toes. "They come to me for everything. I bail them out, I give them advice, I save them. But you know what, they don't know much about me, or at least me before coming to Edenville. If they did, they'd say you and I had a lot in common."

"I doubt that." Willow snickered, and then let her face fall serious as she saw the look of remembering in Michael's eyes. "Or maybe we do, what do I know? I'm starting to realize everyone has a story. Some people just don't like to tell theirs."

"Forget I said anything. I just wanted you to know, I think what you did for Crystal is an amazing thing.

176

You're giving her back a piece of her family she's been missing all these years. You changed lives. Doesn't that feel good?"

"Amazing. I don't think I've ever expected anything like it in my life."

"It's almost curative for the soul. Almost. That's why I don't bring up my own past. I don't need to. You do enough things like you did for Crystal, and those memories start taking up more room in your mind than any of the bad ones. You conjure them up when your eyes are closed and you're about to fall asleep at night. That look on Crystal's face when you told her. It will stick with you more than any of the other things."

"That would be nice," Willow said, hanging her head and kicking at a shell beneath her sandal.

"I screwed things up once with Jules, you know. She took off for the city and I didn't go after her. I thought the adult thing to do was to give her some space, but turns out being an adult is overrated. Don't think like a grown up, that's when we all start getting into trouble, when we over think it."

"Really? Because I was thinking that maybe I should just let him go for a while. Space isn't a good idea?"

"I don't think it is. Even when people say it's what they want, I'm not sure it's a good idea. I'm not talking about tackling him tonight and forcing him to forgive you. But I don't think that letting him go completely is a good idea either. Now," Michael shifted on his feet, "I am drunk so maybe you should filter this advice a bit. Apparently, after you have kids you can't hold your alcohol quite as well. Maybe ask someone else. Hey Piper," Michael yelled, flagging his friend over.

"That is amazing Willow. I can't believe you did

that. Thank you so much for telling her, all of us, tonight. I'm so glad you didn't wait." There was a small slur in her speech that showed she'd been partaking in the spirits of the celebration.

"I was really afraid I was infringing on your special day."

"That kind of thing is right up our alley. I'm dying to know how it goes on the phone. I love when things come together like that. It's so—"

"Redeeming." Willow said, filling in the pause as Piper searched for the right word.

"Exactly."

Jules strode up, stumbled a bit and she caught herself on her husband's arm. "Did you hear that Michael. Crystal's sister is in Ohio. Maybe you and I can go out there with her and Jedda when they're ready. We can finally make the trip to meet your family."

"You haven't met his family yet?" Willow asked, casting a curious look over at Michael who'd just accidently dropped a mysterious bomb about his past.

"Timing just hasn't been right." Michael cut in, keeping his face level. "I don't know if you've heard but hanging around with these knuckleheads keeps a guy pretty busy. We'll get out to meet my folks soon."

As Jules and Piper leaned on each other and laughed at some joke Willow and Michael had missed, she took her opportunity to call his bluff.

"You're hiding something," Willow whispered, narrowing her eyes with accusation.

"Have a drink Willow," Michael insisted as he popped off the top of a beer and shoved it at her. "It's a party, loosen up."

## *Chapter Twenty-Six*

The next morning everyone pulled their sluggish bodies out of bed and out to the water to take in their last deep breaths of sea air before heading home. Betty had cooked a huge breakfast that most of them were to hung over to even smell, so while the parents all partook, the rest of them escaped the smells and congregated with their toes in the sand.

"That was the perfect wedding," Jules sighed, wrapping her arms around Michael's waist.

"It's too bad about your honeymoon," Jedda said as he laced his fingers with Crystal's. She hadn't stopped smiling since she came back to the bonfire last night to report how amazing it was to hear her sister's voice. Crystal called her parents, and while her sister wasn't ready to talk to them herself, they were overjoyed for the news that she was safe. They'd all raised their glasses, threw back shots of one alcohol or another and celebrated the gift that was a happy ending to a difficult story. Which is why they were all hurting this morning.

"It's just a honeymoon" Bobby shrugged, kissing Piper's hand. "I've got everything I need right here."

"I think I'd be too hung over for a honeymoon right now."

"I hope not." Willow laughed as she caught Josh's eye, wishing he'd stop ignoring her this morning. "Denny called your captain. He had a lot of good things to say about you and asked if you'd be available to help on a case for another week. This coming week actually."

"What kind of case?" Bobby asked, looking skeptically at a grinning Willow.

Danielle Stewart

"They have a lead on a cold case that came up in the Cayman Island. He'd like you to go down there and blend in with the tourists. He thinks you'd do even better if you looked like you were really on vacation. Like with your new wife. They'll cover the plane tickets and your hotel. He said the leads a long shot, like a real long shot."

"Are you serious?" Piper asked, jumping up and down and then immediately regretting the fast movement.

"You guys could leave as early as tomorrow morning if you accept the assignment," Willow confirmed with a smile as she tucked her wind-blown hair behind her ear.

"Willow," Bobby said, looking hopeful but guarded. "You really didn't have to do that. We don't regret spending my vacation time up in the city with you."

"I didn't do anything. I mentioned it to Denny and the next morning he was setting it up. He really liked you. He could see you were a good cop and a good friend."

"This is amazing." Piper laid her hand on her aching head. "We need to pack and get someone to watch the house. We'll have a million things to do."

"I was going to ask if you wouldn't mind if I stayed there while you were gone. I've brought back all my parents' old things from their house and Jedda's going to go through it with me."

"So you're staying in Edenville?" Jules asked, with a hopeful look in her eye. "We'd sure love having you."

"I'm not really sure what I'm going to do. I'm going to take it one day at a time and hope something just works out. I know I always have a place on Block Island to go back to. That's a good feeling. Eventually, I want to go back to the apartment and go inside. It's not going to be easy but I need to do it."

180

"You'll do it when you're ready," Piper said, flashing a knowing smile. "You're welcome to stay at our house as long as you'd like. Not just while we're gone. As long as you don't mind dogs. Bruno is good company."

"I appreciate it." Willow nodded; happy Bobby and Piper would be getting their honeymoon.

Josh had been silent through the entire conversation, though most of the eyes in the group had glanced over at him every time Willow spoke. Willow however had tried to not stare at him. It was a feat that took most of her willpower.

"Everything's cleaned up from last night. I'm heading back to town now. You need me to put anything in my car?" Josh asked as he pulled his keys from his pocket.

Everyone froze for a moment, looking uncomfortable and disappointed by the idea that Willow and Josh hadn't patched things up. He wasn't blatantly ignoring her but the tension was easy to see.

"I think we have enough space," Michael said, shooting a steely stare at Willow. "Don't you think so Willow, more than enough space? Probably too much really." Apparently Michael hadn't been too drunk to remember his advice from last night and Willow was hearing his message loud and clear, but she couldn't find the words that would win her Josh's forgiveness.

"Okay then," Josh said awkwardly as he waved and headed back up to the house to say goodbye.

"You need a big move Willow," Michael implored, urging her with his eyes to go after Josh.

"It's not the right time. I'm not giving up but I know he's not ready to hear what I have to say yet. You guys don't understand how badly I screwed this up. It's going to take time."

"You're preaching to the screw-up choir," Betty laughed as she joined them out on the beach and wrapped her arm around Willow's shoulder. "Don't worry too much, your mama is in there right now, trying to convince Josh that you're worth another shot."

"Oh my gosh," Willow cried making a move for the house, but Betty's arms snared her in place.

"She's your mama, that's her job. Let her do her work child."

"That's mortifying, is everyone in there just standing around listening to her make her case?"

"Yup." Betty grinned as Willow rested her pink cheek on her shoulder.

Everyone broke into an empathetic laughter as they made their way down closer to the water taking in the last few waves against their feet before they were forced back to reality. Only Crystal stayed behind and Betty finally released Willow, touching both girls on the shoulder and tipping her head with a warm smile. "I'm so glad to have you two here. I feel like your lives were meant to intersect in North Carolina. It's not always easy to believe that everything happens for a reason. But moments like last night, it restores your faith a little doesn't it?"

"It sure does," Crystal chimed in reaching her hand across to Willow. She'd never really grown accustomed to a lot of physical touching from people, but she took Crystal's hand anyway and squeezed it tightly.

Betty stepped away quietly to join everyone else who was staring peacefully out at the horizon.

"I don't know if thank you will ever be enough,"

Crystal said, releasing Willow's hand and taking a seat on one of the chairs around the now extinguished fire.

"This changed me Crystal, it really did. I feel so different now that I actually did something that matters. Something that worked out. You don't need to thank me. I've already gotten so much out of this experience."

"My family was destroyed Willow. That's not an exaggeration. Getting Erica back, that's a gift we'd long since given up on. In our minds, just finding out what had happened to her, getting her body back, getting some closure was what we'd resigned ourselves to as a best case scenario. When so much time goes by you get too afraid to let yourself believe you might get good news. I think I'm still in shock."

"I bet she is, too. What did it feel like talking to her last night?" Willow wanted as much detail as Crystal was willing to share. It was like Michael had said; you only have room for so many memories in your mind. She was trying to fill herself to the brim with happy ones, pushing anything else out of the way.

"It was so strange, I thought it would be awkward but really it was as though no time at all had past. Her voice was the same. She was still my sister. Hearing that she was happy and safe, that she'd found her way in this world was amazing. But the most important thing she said to me was that none of this would have been possible without you."

Willow averted her eyes from Crystal as she took a seat on the chair next to her. "It took a lot of people working to get it to come together."

"She told me the truth Willow. She didn't want to see me. It hurt to hear but I'm starting to realize that her life has been complicated. Her exact words were, if

Willow hadn't been so convincing I don't think I would have had the courage to do this. It never crossed my mind that it would take courage to reconnect with me, but it's all starting to make sense. She was truly afraid, and you did something to sway her. I'll forever be grateful for that"

"I told her everything," Willow voice cracked "I told her my own story, in detail that I've never done before. Memories I'd forbidden myself from speaking again. I tore out my own heart and showed her how broken it is, but that it was still beating."

Crystal's hand came up to her mouth as she crumpled, shedding what would likely be her millionth tear over the last twelve hours. "Thank you, Willow. That must have been so–"

"Therapeutic," Willow explained as she reached across and placed her hand on Crystal's shoulder. "I told you, this changed me. I needed this so badly."

"And now what will you do?"

"I have no clue. For the first time, I'm realizing I really am welcomed in so many places. There's a home for me, all I have to do is be ready to take it. Did Jedda tell you about all the stuff in my rental car? I have boxes from the apartment we grew up in. We're going to go through it. Maybe when we get back to Edenville. Do you think that would be too much for him? You know him better than anyone right now. You know how he's doing with therapy."

"He has good days and bad. Some days he's angry, some days he's sad. I think going through those boxes might be hard but it will help you both in the end. I do have one suggestion though," Crystal reasoned. "You may want to consider doing it here. Edenville is his soft place to fall right now. It's where he's working. It's where he's healing. Bringing those memories past that city line, might be unhealthy for him."

"I never thought of that. Do you think we should do it here, this morning? Like now?"

"You've got a couple hours before we have to head out. If you think you're up to it doing it this morning would probably be best."

"I'm up to it. I'll head out to the car and carry the boxes out here. Do you mind asking Jedda if he's ready? And everyone, if they don't mind could be here with us." Willow lit up as she got to her feet, feeling completely prepared to dive headfirst into this small pool of her past. Completely prepared knowing she wouldn't be alone in the water.

She walked swiftly toward the car, an anxious skip in her step as she rounded the house and saw Josh sitting in his car. The engine was running but he didn't seem to be going anywhere. He didn't see her, his gaze fixed ahead of him, so she tapped lightly on his window.

"You okay?" she asked through the closed window as he shook himself back to reality. He rolled the window down and rubbed at the tension in his temple.

"I'm good, just thinking before I take off."

"About what?"

"Whether or not I'm ready to hear what you have to say. I'm genuinely happy that you've started heading in the right direction. I just want to stand next to you and watch you get yourself together. But I'm still pissed. You walked away, and if Marcario hadn't been killed out there, would you be here right now? I don't like the answer I keep coming up with to that question. So what does that mean the next time something goes wrong?"

185

"I don't know," Willow admitted, her two hands on the frame of his car window, clinging to it as though it were her last connection to him.

"I think it's good that you'll admit that anyway," he responded, gripping his steering wheel tightly. "I'd be more worried if you were sitting here promising me that it will never happen again. That you've got everything under control now and you're not planning to live your life with your running shoes on."

"I hope I'm not, but I think it's too soon to say. I don't feel like running away right now, but that doesn't mean I never will."

"I guess I'm not really one to judge the running. I'm feeling like running myself lately. You've kind of ruined Edenville for me."

"I did?" Willow asked, furrowing her brows and biting at her lip guiltily.

"Maybe that's a little dramatic. I just mean that I was already feeling a little caged in there, now the more I've seen of the world the less Edenville feels like home to me. It just feels too insulated, too blind to what's really going on. I just want more."

"I won't make you any promises Josh, because that would be selfish and reckless. Two things I'm trying to be less of. But I'd really like if you stayed. I was coming out to get the boxes you packed up for me from the apartment. Jedda and I are going to go through them this morning. Crystal doesn't think bringing them to Edenville is a great idea. That's Jedda's safe place and keeping the two things separate could be helpful."

"That makes sense," Josh nodded, looking like he was arguing with himself about what to do next. "I wanted to tell you earlier, while there might be something in there that means something to you, there wasn't anything in there that would be really catastrophic to see. It was all pretty straightforward stuff. In case you were worried."

"Thanks, I was worried. Well, worried and a little hopeful that maybe there'd be something in there I could give to Denny and he could chase down more leads. But even if there isn't I'll still be glad to be done with all of it." Willow fidgeted with the zipper on her sweatshirt and waited for Josh to make a move to get out of the car. "I know I blew it with you Josh, but I could really use you as my friend again. No one's ever understood me like you do. The real me, the one I didn't even understand."

"Let's get those boxes in," Josh sighed, clearly trying to look more reluctant than he was. "I do understand you, Willow. That's not to say it doesn't scare the hell out of me, but I do understand you."

"Well we have that in common at least. Finally understanding myself is scaring the shit out of me too."

## *Chapter Twenty-Seven*

"Light the fire," Jedda insisted as he stacked a pile of his old things up in his lap. "Make it a roaring one Bobby, because I want to watch all this stuff burn."

"Are you sure?" Crystal asked holding up an old shirt that must have been Jedda's when he was smaller.

"I'm positive." Willow had gone through most of the things that had belonged to her and was starting to agree with Jedda's plan. Burning it felt right.

Piper, Jules, and Betty stepped back into the circle around the fire pit on the beach. They'd just seen the last of the guests off and now it was just this small group left. Frankie was down for a nap and Betty had the baby monitor clipped to her apron pocket.

"Looks like y'all are making progress. Find anything interesting?"

"Lots of memories, that's for sure. Clothes, some stuffed animals, and a few books." Willow pointed at each pile. "Nothing I was hoping for really."

"And what were you hoping for?" Betty asked as she took a seat next to Willow. "Oh hello there Josh, thought you'd left. Good to see you thought better of being an idiot. I like to see that."

Everyone snickered as Josh rolled his eyes. "Willow was thinking she might find something she could give to the police in Jersey so they could investigate her parents' crimes further. So far nothing." Josh had answered the question and ignored Betty's snipe, though the look they exchanged followed by a smile from both of them let Willow know it hadn't been missed.

"What's this?" Jules asked, leaning down and

picking up a navy colored book with a loaf of bread drawn on the front.

"A cook book," Jedda said seeming to give it no attention at all as Jules flipped through the pages.

"These are all hand written, did your mother cook? Were these her recipes?"

Willow let out a loud and dramatic laugh. "My mother never cooked a day in her life that I know of. That must be someone else's."

At that Jedda took more interest, wondering if maybe it was something that could connect Willow and him to someone else in their past. Grandparents they never met? "Can I see it?" Jedda asked and Jules tossed it across the newly lit fire into his lap.

He flipped intently through the pages, as everyone seemed to go on to other conversations and stoked the fire. But Willow's eyes were locked on Jedda. The expression on her brother's face was keeping her fixed on him, and Josh was tuning into her as well.

"What is it?" Josh asked in a hushed voice, leaning into Willow. The smell of his cologne wafted across her, carried by the sea air and it calmed the fear growing in her.

"This is her handwriting. Mom's. She wrote all these out." Jedda said, flipping through each page. "It doesn't make any sense. She didn't cook. Ever. Why would she have all these hand written recipes?"

"Hand it here Jedda," Betty requested, slipping her reading glasses on. "There's got to be fifty recipes here. Who would hand write all of these out if they didn't cook? That doesn't make any sense." She scrutinized the first few recipes with a grimace on her face. "Well no one could cook any of these."

"What do you mean?" Willow asked a knot tightening in her throat. "Are they recipes or not?"

"They're written like recipes, but you couldn't cook anything edible with them. The ingredients don't line up with anything. This recipe is for tamales, but none of the ingredients makes sense. There are no apples in tamales that's for sure."

"Can I see it?" Willow asked urgently, practically snatching the book from Betty's hands. She scanned the page looking for anything that might pull all of this together. "Look the recipes are dated, no one does that. This could be their records of what they were doing with girls. This is a Spanish recipe. The cheese is aged, thirteen years. Could that be describing a person? It says it yields ten servings, maybe that's the price?"

"That seems like a pretty big leap Willow," Bobby cautioned, coming around behind her and leaning over her shoulder.

"Well they aren't recipes," Betty insisted. "They're certainly written to hide something. I don't see why it couldn't be that."

"Bobby," Willow said, flipping the page to the date she recalled from their research in the city. "This is the date that Josephine was taken. Look at the recipe. It's all her information. The date, her age, it's all on this page. These could be their records. We'd have something to give Denny that he could actually work with." She was on her feet and shoving the book in Bobby's face before anyone could get a word out.

"If it were some kind of record book of the girls they abducted and sold it could certainly help close a lot of open cases." Bobby agreed as he took the book from Willow's shaking hands and started looking it over. "This could be a significant piece of evidence."

"Don't you people ever just have a normal event? You just got married, and you're already looking for new trouble," a voice from behind the group said with a hardy laugh that had everyone turning to face the man.

Willow pulled the book back from Bobby and held it close to her chest. The arrival of a stranger at such a crucial moment was unsettling to her and she felt the urge to protect the book.

"Christian Donavan?" Josh asked, with a look that made the hair on the back of Willow's neck stand up.

It wasn't until Bobby and Piper's face broke into wide smiles that couldn't be mistaken for anything but true joy that Willow relaxed.

"Christian, I mean Chris," Piper corrected. "What are you doing here?"

"The two tortured souls finally smarten up and get married? I wouldn't miss that for the world."

Danielle Stewart

## Chapter Twenty-Eight

Piper couldn't believe her eyes when Christian appeared on the beach out of nowhere. He'd been a person who'd from the first time they met could see right through her bullshit, straight to the truth. It was annoying at times of course but usually he was the kick in the ass she needed to get back on track.

"So how do you guys know each other," Willow asked, still clutching the book in her hands tightly.

"It's a long story," Chris quipped. "A really long story. But we met a while back when we were all trying to either save our asses or save the world. I live out in Illinois with my new wife, my brother, and my son. I used to live in Edenville but," Chris turned toward Bobby with a devilish grin as he asked, "she's okay right? I mean she's one of you guys?"

"She's one of us," Piper assured him with a wink at Willow.

"Well then I guess I can tell you I used to live in Edenville until I sold out everyone I worked with and went into witness protection. I was the save my ass part of that equation."

"No you weren't," Piper shot back, waving him off. "You helped bring down some very deplorable people on your way out of town. You saved my life, and I don't mean that metaphorically. He actually saved my life," Piper explained, turning toward Jedda, Crystal and Willow. The only ones who didn't know the story of how her father nearly killed her until Chris came in and killed him before he could finish Piper off.

"You had a pretty notorious reputation in Edenville,"

192

Josh chimed in with a hint of attitude that said he still wasn't convinced of Chris's conversion to a good guy.

"Reputations are often blown out of proportion." Chris said, grabbing a stick and poking at the fire.

"Was yours?" Willow asked, still not completely adjusted to biting her tongue when it was necessary.

"Nope." Chris admitted, catching the end of his stick on fire and then stomping it out under his shoe.

"Chris got married in Vegas last month," Bobby cut in, changing the subject as he passed him a beer from the cooler. "Where's the new wife?"

"It was harder than you think to come out here. You'd be amazed how little the feds appreciate you trying to go back to the state they pulled you out of. I knew I couldn't be here for the ceremony, but I figured I could catch you before you headed back to Edenville. Unfortunately Sydney and little Chris are back in Illinois."

"How's Sean doing?" Betty asked and Piper tried to remind herself that even if Sean had started out as a complete jackass, Chris's brother had worked hard to reform his old ways.

"Doing great. He's been sober since he came out of rehab and he's still doing therapy twice a week. He starts a new job at the beginning of the month. I'm really proud of him." The look in Christian's eye was so paternal that Piper couldn't fight a smirk. They'd all come so far, and worked damn hard to get happy. That was the strangest lesson of Piper's life so far. Happy was hard work.

"There's another reason Sydney couldn't come," Chris hinted as he took a long swig of his beer, leaving everyone in suspense. "The morning sickness is killing her."

Danielle Stewart

"What?" Betty hooted almost knocking Willow off the small bench they were sharing. "Congratulations. Oh, the babies! I can't wait for all these babies. Next thing you know it'll be Bobby and Piper."

"Not us," Piper insisted, regretting the timing of her statement. She and Bobby had a well thought out plan of when to talk about their choice not to have their own children. But like usual Piper's mouth didn't check with her brain before she spoke.

"What does that mean?" Jules questioned, as though Piper had just spoken some foreign language.

"We're doing this now?" Bobby asked, and Piper gave an apologetic shrug of her shoulders.

"I guess we are," she answered, straightening herself up. "We've decided we are going to adopt when we're ready to start a family. I've never really pictured myself having children. Until I met Bobby, I never thought I'd get married. The more I considered what the rest of my life might be like, the more I realized I'd want to adopt. It just feels right with everything we've been through. There are so many kids out there who need someone to love them. If Bobby and I adopted them, look at all the people they'd get."

"But you wouldn't have any kids of your own?" Betty asked looking like she'd just been struck by tsunami.

"No. We wouldn't" Bobby answered firmly, sliding his hand into Piper's as a silent show of solidarity.

"I've never heard anything like that," Betty grimaced as Clay reached out and touched her shoulder gently. His caress was enough to remind Betty that sometimes people need to make their own choices So Betty pulled her face into a smile. "But every child deserves love. If this is

194

what you two want to do, I can't think of anyone better to do it."

"Thank you," Piper stuttered, letting the tears in her eyes spill over. "I know it's not normal."

"If I was expecting normal I'd go out shopping for all new people to spend time with," Betty laughed as she pulled them both in for a hug. "Whatever you do, we'll be here for you."

"Never a dull moment with you guys," Chris huffed sarcastically as he took a seat on one of the chairs by the fire. "But that's what I like about you. So tell me what's in this book? I want in."

"I knew you couldn't help yourself," Michael shot back as he tossed another beer in Chris's direction.

"Can you blame me? She's holding that book like it's got a treasure map in it. I'm intrigued. I've been out of the game too long. I need to be in on another crazy scheme."

"You've come to the right place," Piper retorted as she took stock of the people around her. Everyone in this circle had done the heavy lifting that came with real love. They'd worked. Begged for forgiveness. Accepted apologies. Embraced each other's flaws.

Though all their relationships worked for very different reasons, Piper's own life with Bobby was what gave her hope for Willow and Josh. Bobby had to work harder than anyone, not just to win Piper's affection but to convince her she was worthy of his. Of anyone's really. She saw so much of herself in Willow, though Bobby would likely disagree. They both harbored a similar pain, but they handled it differently. Piper built a wall around herself, and she learned to live behind it. Willow on the other hand didn't need the wall. She relied on lashing out, launching attacks on people foolish enough to see the real her. It made Willow seem much more hostile than Piper, but in reality, they were both nursing a similar brokenness.

Piper hadn't torn down her own wall completely; she found small openings to let people in. If Willow could control the urge to snipe anyone who got close, and Josh was strong enough to keep trying when she failed, then there truly was hope for them.

## Chapter Twenty-Nine

"I can't believe you guys rented this house out for another night," Bobby chuckled as he loaded Piper's bags into the back of his truck. It was adorned with tin cans and a hand painted just married sign in the back window.

"We've got a lot of work to do." Michael said with a forced seriousness as he waved at Betty and Clay who were pulling out of the driveway with Frankie in the back seat.

"Oh please, you're just happy to have a night without the baby." Jules retorted as she drove an elbow playfully into her husband's side.

"Guilty as charged," Michael admitted as he leaned in and scooped Jules off of her feet. Spinning her around as he kissed at her neck. "We'll be in the master suite. No one bother us." He tossed Jules over his shoulder like a sack of potatoes and disappeared back into the house.

Willow found herself holding her breath every time another car pulled out. It was another opportunity for Josh to announce he was leaving too. When she'd left the group that morning to call Denny and tell him about the book, she was sure when she got back he'd be gone. But he wasn't. When they'd all decided to stay an extra night to help organize the information in the book and take a second look at all the other belongings taken from the apartment of Willow's biological parents she thought Josh would use that chance to say he was leaving, but he didn't.

As she watched Michael and Jules playfully enter the house, and Bobby and Piper hop in the car to head out as husband and wife, she found herself thinking only of

Josh. She'd taken Michael's advice and done something big, something that ignored any request for space. Now it was time to see if it would work.

"Can I talk to you for a second Willow," Jedda asked just as she intended to pose the same question to Josh. The look in Jedda's eyes was enough to keep her from being able to turn him down.

"Of course," she acquiesced as she watched Josh fish his keys out of his pocket. "Don't go," she said catching his arm with urgency that had everyone's eyes fixed on her.

"I was just going to pull my car up," Josh smiled awkwardly. "I had to move my car to let Bobby and Piper out, I was just going to pull it back in."

"Oh, yeah, go do that," Willow stammered as she tried to casually shrug the embarrassment off.

"We'll bring the boxes in so you can go through them again and see if you overlooked anything," Crystal said, trailing off as she and Chris headed for the house, and Josh headed for his car.

"I feel like we haven't talked," Jedda said, leaning himself against Chris's rental car.

"I think I was avoiding you," Willow admitted as she cast her eyes guiltily away from him.

"Why?" Jedda asked with a pain in his eye that hurt Willow even more. He had a look on his face as though he'd done something wrong and that couldn't be further from the truth.

"I've done a lot of selfish stupid things over the last couple of months, well years maybe. But of everything I regret, the way I treated you kills me the most."

"You were hurt and confused. I don't fault you for feeling how you did," Jedda insisted, lifting her chin with one finger and upturning her face so their eyes met. "I've tried to work really hard in therapy and part of it was trying to understand why you were so angry with me. It's survivor's guilt Willow."

"But we both survived," she said not letting the out he was giving her penetrate her self-hate for how she'd treated him.

"You saw my going to prison as a form of death. It's normal to go through all the emotions you have. Including being angry with me."

"That's the stupidest thing I've ever done. Do you know when it hit me, how absolutely foolish I was being? When I got a chance to see how other girls in the same position as me turned out. If only someone had been able to save them the way you saved me. I'm so lucky you were willing to kill for me. I'm so grateful and so very sorry it took me this long to understand it." Willow had worked through these words, well more concise words, for over a week. She had every intention of this sounding better, of them being somewhere other than standing outside leaning on a car. It was meant to be more powerful, more profound. But the message seemed to be registering with Jedda.

"I don't regret it. I've told you that. I've always just wanted you to be happy and safe. I would do it all over again." Jedda choked out as he pulled Willow against him, squeezing her in a hug that nearly crushed her.

"I'm going to do better. I'm going to be better. I've been a bitch to everyone."

"You don't have to be, not all at once. I think you'd be promising the impossible."

"How's anyone going to ever forgive me, or care about me the way I am right now? The way I've been?"

"Wake up Willow, they already do. They might not like the way you've acted, but they love you in spite of it. I know it's not how we grew up when we were little, and it's hard to believe that it really exists but it does. There really are people who can love no matter what. And that's more powerful than anything we've been through. It's bigger than our past."

"I'm going to put it all out there for Josh. I'm terrified he's going to tell me to go to hell."

"He might," Jedda shrugged as he released Willow from his tight grip. "Or maybe he might not. You never know until you do it."

"Why did you forgive Crystal? She misled you. She kept a secret from you. You were finally opening yourself up. How did you get past that?"

"I'd already lost so many years of my life. Here was someone that was more like me than I had realized. She was willing to risk everything. I know what that decision is like and I respect what she was doing, even if it hurt me at the time."

"Maybe Josh will feel like that?"

"You were being kind of a jerk," Jedda said through a snickering laugh, then quickly straightening his face. "But he's a good guy and he seems like he can see the forest for through your crazy ass trees."

"I hope so."

"Now's your chance to find out," Jedda said raising an eyebrow in Josh's direction as he approached. He leaned in and kissed Willow's cheek as he whispered, "You're my baby sister. No matter what happens with Josh, I'll always be here for you."

Rather than just accept his kiss and let him go, she wrapped her arms around his neck and pulled him into her to the point where he nearly lost his footing.

After a moment, as Josh's footsteps grew closer, Jedda wiggled out of her grip and winked at her.

She sucked in her bottom lip as the tears trailed freely down her cheeks. Jedda's love had saved her. It wasn't a burden to be saved it was a miracle.

"You okay?" Josh asked as he stepped in close to Willow and then leaned back on his heels to put safe distance between them.

"Just a lot of tough conversations and overdue realizations on my part. It's not easy figuring out you're an asshole."

"You're not, well acting like one and being one are two different things."

"Josh I know that you said you didn't want to do this here. You said you wanted space to figure things out. I can't give you space. I'm sorry."

"What do you mean?"

"I'm too afraid to give you space, like if I give you enough time you'll figure out you're too good for me. So I'm just going to put it out there and pray you will listen."

"I don't think that's a—"

"I don't care," Willow insisted as she drew in a deep breath. "I called Denny this morning. He's anxious to get a hold of the book. He did some quick cross-referencing of information I read to him and he thinks it could be a huge source of information on open cases. He asked me to go up there. My experience with the cases gives me a unique advantage and I could consult."

"And that's what you want to do?"

"I talked to my parents. Since I put them through the ringer lately, I thought I'd better see how they feel about it first. They were worried but supportive."

"So when do you go?"

"That depends on what you say," Willow croaked out timidly, knowing that once these words were spoken they couldn't be taken back.

"Last I checked you didn't answer to me. If you want to go there and help out on these cases, then you should."

"I know I don't answer to you," Willow snarled back and then bit her tongue remembering she was the one who should be receiving the attitude right now. She deserved anything Josh wanted to throw at her. "I want you to come with me. I already bought you a ticket for Thursday."

"You bought me a plane ticket?" Josh asked, his mouth agape. "After I told you I wanted time?"

"Yes," Willow admitted apologetically. "I know it was crazy. You have your practice and you've lived here your whole life. This could take months, maybe even a year. But if you don't want to come, it's okay. I can just make copies and mail the book up to Denny and we can stay here."

"Edenville isn't home for you, you know that."

"I can be happy anywhere if you're there. I'll cancel the tickets and we can just stay. I just want to be where you are."

"How am I supposed to trust that? Am I going to wake up every morning and wonder if you're going to be there? That's no way to live."

"I have literally no answer for you. I feel like running right now. When I sat down with my parents, I wanted to run. When Jedda just asked to talk to me, I wanted run. I don't know how to turn that off. And I don't want to lie about it either. I just know I can't imagine going somewhere and you not being there."

"Tell me why. I need to hear why you think you want me in your life." Josh was firm faced and teetering on the verge of anger.

Willow didn't have an immediate answer. The urge was just to say she loved him and hope that would be enough, but she knew that was cheating. That wasn't what he meant. So in usual Willow fashion she tried to think about what he'd expect her to say. Just like she'd done with every therapist, her adoptive parents, Brad, and a whole host of others. Then she realized that, within itself was her answer. "You're the first person who doesn't have an expectation of my perfection, of me being healed or saved. You haven't asked me to be anything other than what I am. Before I completely blew it with you, somehow you loved these jagged edges of me that I'd always tried to hide, and everyone else had ignored. You didn't try to dig up the best in me, you saw the worst and you still loved me. I think I need that in my life, and I don't think I'll ever find it again the same way I had it with you."

Josh drew in a deep breath and scratched tiredly at his head. "That's a damn good answer."

"It's the truth," Willow said simply, finally able to bring her gaze up to Josh's.

"Edenville doesn't feel like home to me either," Josh sighed as he ran a finger across Willow's cheek. The warmth of his touch brought tears back to her eyes. "I can bring on some partners at the practice and have them run it while I'm gone. I've had some great offers over the years. That's the nice part of being the only show in town."

"And you can see yourself in the city? I don't know how these cases are going to go, it might be a lot of bad news over and over again."

"I'm tired of living in this bubble and pretending everything in the world is perfect. I love being a doctor and helping people, but I feel like I'm only scratching the surface of what I could be doing. I want to go with you."

"Just because you don't want to be in Edenville?" Willow asked, knowing full well, her wide eyes were begging for him to quench her thirst with a drop of his love.

"No," he said, giving in, "not just because I want to leave Edenville. I want to be wherever you are." He spun her around and brushed her cheek with the back of his hand as he pressed her against the car she was leaning on. The full weight of his body making her feel completely safe. "I want to go wherever you are, if you'd just stay there long enough for me to love you."

"I promise to try," Willow whispered as Josh leaned in close, his lips just inches from hers. "Thank you for not giving up on me." Their lips met and Willow felt her heart swell as his hands tightened around her waist. She lost herself in the kiss, let it bowl her over like a wave and instead of fighting to get her footing, she let it take her to shore.

Josh broke the kiss and looked down into her face tentatively searching for something he might be able to latch onto. She could see him convincing himself that Willow was worth the gamble, and it pained her to know she'd made that necessary.

"I'm proud of the things you've been doing here Willow," he said leaning in and kissing her forehead. "I believe in you."

And just like that, Josh became the thread that mended her split seams and repaired her frayed edges. He pulled the loose piece of her back together and she knew that the promise she was making was one she could keep. She could be better.

Danielle Stewart

## *Six Weeks Later*

"How's it been going, working all the cases with Denny?" Bobby asked Willow as he bent down and laced up his sneaker. His skin was still tan from his working vacation with Piper.

"No big wins yet but, some great leads. He actually has surveillance on two men that I identified through mug shots as having dealt with my parents. That's been promising." Willow said as she stared up at the door of the apartment building she'd been held captive in.

"Well, you look well considering Josh tells me you've been busier than a one eyed cat watching a dozen rat holes," Betty teased looking her up and down.

"He's been busy too. He's working at the clinic next to our new apartment. He's making a real difference there," Willow bragged with a smile as she took Josh's hand. "Thank you all for coming. I can't believe you all got here." Willow took a look at the group that had gathered. Her people: her adoptive parents, Piper and Bobby, Michael and Jules, Betty and Clay, and Jedda and Crystal were all standing on the lawn of a terrible place, and their simple presence stole some of the power it had over her.

Betty pushed the stray pieces of her wind-blown hair aside as she smiled hopefully at Willow. "Are you doing any singing? I sure love your voice. I'd hate to see you rob the world of it."

"I've taken a little break from singing while I help out up here. When I go back to it I want it to be with a clear head."

"I had the chance to meet with Denny yesterday to

206

thank him personally for helping to find Erica," Crystal said, touching Willow's trembling arm gently. "You left something out of the story. He told me you paid the witness for the information. Out of your own pocket and it wasn't a small amount."

"I got some money from a friend who died out in California. He wanted me to use it in a way that helped me get on with my life. I initially thought I should take it and pay my parents back but when I told them what I did with the money they understood. I'd do it again tomorrow given the chance."

"I know I've said it a hundred times before, but thank you," Crystal gulped as she leaned backward into Jedda's arms.

"You ready?" Josh asked, taking a step toward the entrance where Tony was waiting to let them into the apartment.

"As I'll ever be," whispered Willow as she met his stride and headed toward the door. She turned back to see the legion of people who'd gathered to support her as she faced the darkest place she'd ever known. It was clear to her now, this was a place where bad things had happened to her, but they weren't happening anymore. This, all these people behind her, that was happening now.

She stepped inside the door, farther in now than any other attempt she'd made and as the smell hit her nose, she felt like she was falling from the clouds, plummeting toward the earth. That was okay though because there were plenty of people to catch her.

*Epilogue*

As they stood staring up at the run down somber looking apartment that Willow had just stepped into Michael's phone rang. It drew everyone's attention and elicited a roll of Jules's emerald green eyes. "I swear your office doesn't know what the word vacation means," she huffed as she released his hand and he stepped away, an apology on his tongue.

After nearly ten minutes, Bobby wondered why Michael hadn't been able to get off the phone with whoever had called. Clearly Jules was wondering the same thing as she griped, "The whole point of us being here was to support Willow when she comes out if she needs us and he's going to be on the phone."

"Go get him Bobby," Betty said shoving him in the direction Michael had disappeared to.

"I'll go with you," Piper said, tugging a reluctant Bobby along. "He's probably micromanaging whatever cases he left behind."

As he and Piper rounded the corner of the adjacent building, they saw Michael bracing himself against the brick wall as though he'd just taken a physical blow. "What happened?" Piper asked, racing toward him as he instantly tried to gather himself. It was too late; they'd already seen his crumpled over shoulders and the pain in his face.

"That was my mom," Michael blurted out with a cracking in his voice. "My dad had a heart attack. He's dead."

"I'm so sorry," Piper opened her arms to him but he didn't move toward her. He straightened his back and swallowed hard.

"I need to get to Ohio."

"Of course," Bobby said, as though it was the only thing that made sense. "Do you want Piper and me to keep Frankie while you and Jules go?"

"No, I'm going by myself," Michael insisted as he tucked his phone back in his pocket. "Tell Jules," he hesitated on the words, clearly struggling to come up with a message. "Tell her I'm sorry, and I'll be back in Edenville by the weekend."

"Wait a second," Bobby said catching his arm as he spun to leave. "We've all turned a blind eye to the fact that you don't talk about your family. It's none of our business that up until this point they haven't met your wife or daughter. But I'll be damned if I'm going to walk back up to my friend and tell her that her father-in-law just died and her husband took off without her."

"You don't understand Bobby. I've stood by all of you with your stuff, I'm asking you to do the same."

"No, you're not, Michael," Piper snapped. "You're not asking us to stand by you, you're asking us to watch you bail. You're married now. You exchanged vows, for better or worse. Whatever it is, she'll understand."

"I don't like this new optimistic Piper, she's too happy to remember how messy things can be," Michael said in a hushed and serious voice as he shook his arm free from Bobby's grip.

"Take care of my girls Bobby," Michael called as he hustled toward the street, a pleading look in his eyes.

Bobby wanted to chase after him and tackle him to the ground. He wanted to hold him there and force him to face whatever it was he was running from, or running toward. Instead, when he saw the desperation in his best friend's eyes, so he did the only thing he could, reassure him. "I will," he called back feeling like the earth had just spun off its axis. It had been Michael, Jules, Bobby and Piper for almost two years now. They'd been through hell and back together. This was supposed to be the beginning of their finally peaceful lives. Michael was a husband and father now. He had responsibilities to Jules. Hell, he had responsibilities to all of them. That was who he was, the stable one. He was the voice of reason in the face of everyone else's panic. Now suddenly as he ran away from them at a frantic pace Bobby could tell all of that was about to change.

"What are you saying Bobby?" Piper pleaded anxiously tugging at his arm. "We need to go after him."

"We will, just not yet."


Follow The Piper Anderson Series in book six
Battling Destiny September 2014

Sign up for Danielle Stewart's Mailing List at
www.AuthorDanielleStewart.com

One random newsletter subscriber will be chosen
every month in 2014.  The chosen subscriber will receive
a $25 eGift Card! Sign up today by clicking the link
above

CPSIA information can be obtai
Printed in the USA
LVOW11s0256051015

456906LV00001B/

7 81500 178376